Wall of Solid Mist

Wall of Solid Mist

—— Katriel Hoogsteen ——

RESOURCE *Publications* · Eugene, Oregon

WALL OF SOLID MIST

Resource Publications
An Imprint of Wipf and Stock Publishers
199 W. 8th Ave., Suite 3
Eugene, OR 97401

www.wipfandstock.com

PAPERBACK ISBN: 978-1-7252-8007-6
HARDCOVER ISBN: 978-1-7252-8005-2
EBOOK ISBN: 978-1-7252-8008-3

05/11/21

*For Pake, who always wanted another
writer in the family.*

*For Mike, who told me to "do something"
with my writing ability.
(Satisfied?)*

*And for Haleigh, a source of inspiration
and my literary guinea pig.*

Contents

1

Berry Picking

Skylar

A thick, white mist hangs in the air as I walk along the familiar dirt trail. As always, it's deserted, but I wouldn't expect to see anyone now, even on a main road. It's early, much earlier than when I usually go out. That's Mom's doing. When I got up this morning she told me that she and my sister, Mandy, had used up the rest of the arda berries in their baking yesterday, and if Dad was going to have any bunches of them to sell today I would have to go pick some before breakfast.

I keep reminding myself that everyone needs to make sacrifices when running a family business as I swing my empty reed basket and try not to grumble about the early work the way my stomach is grumbling. I should be grateful, anyway. My family certainly isn't rich, but we're better off than most Mistems. Most of them rely on farming, and the Haeltons often raid farms. Our business means we don't worry as much about things like that, though we still just barely scrape by. That's life for most of us.

My family's business is built on the arda berries I've been sent to gather. Dad goes to the market every day to sell them, both in bunches and in the baked goods Mom and Mandy make with them. My job is the most exciting—getting the berries. It might not sound exciting, but I found a way to change that.

As I near the marshes which give my village, Marshwall, its name, I push a white braid off my shoulder with a pale hand. Pale skin and white hair: the main distinguishing features of a Mistem. My village is mostly populated with Mistems, a quiet, peaceful race. If anyone else knew what

I do to get arda berries, they might faint from the shock. Or maybe not, considering I'm the one doing it.

I reach the hollow log where I hide my most important berry picking tool and pull out the long, thick stick that I carved into a makeshift spear. I test the point with my thumb. It's starting to become a bit dull, but it should still work well enough for today. I'll just have to sneak a knife with me on my next trip to sharpen it.

A fact about arda berries that very few people in my village know is that they grow best in the marshes. Of course, very few people actually go to these marshes. They're known for being a dangerous place. Even Haeltons, the fighting-obsessed warriors and overlords of the Mistems, avoid this place when they can help it. So why would any ever-fearful, over-cautious Mistems ever want to come here? Well, why not? I like to add a bit of excitement in the midst of my dull, restrictive life and this is the only way I can get it.

I scout around the edge of the marsh first, then spot a promising bunch of the round, midnight-blue berries up in one of the many leafy trees that grow on the soft ground where the water is lower. I aim for the stem with my spear, take a breath to steady myself, and launch my projectile in a familiar and well-practiced motion. It misses and lands with a splash a few yards away. Like I said, it's early; I need a warm-up. Holding the hem of my work clothes above my knees so as not to get it wet (I don't need my parents noticing and asking unwanted questions), I wade through the murky water over to where my spear landed. I turn, take aim, and throw again. This time there's a satisfying snap as the spear cuts through the stem and both berries and spear land on the ground beneath the tree. I pick up the arda berries and help myself to a few of them before putting the rest in my basket. They're delicious; the tangy-sweet taste floods my mouth as the skin snaps between my teeth. I can see why our stand in the market is always so popular.

For about half an hour I continue my sport, sometimes doing trick shots with my spear by hanging from branches or launching off tree trunks, throwing in mid-air, and doing flips before landing. My trick shots keep getting more and more elaborate every time I go berry picking. I like adding more challenge whenever I go out.

As the mist dissipates in the wake of the rising sun, I realize I should be heading home soon, especially since my basket is nearly full. I look up at the sky through the intertwining branches of berry trees. It looks like it will be a nice, sunny day. The blue of the sky resembles the colour of my eyes, my one physical feature that isn't typical of a Mistem.

I'm about to pick up my basket and head home when a sound from behind stops me in my tracks—a splash, as if something just came out of the water. I whip around, spear ready in my hand; it isn't just for berry picking. Sure enough, clinging to the trunk of a tree not five yards away from me, beady black eyes staring straight into mine, is one of the creatures that give these marshes their reputation. It's a knightcrawler—a man-sized, lizard-like beast with steel-gray skin that's hard as armour and dagger-sharp claws and teeth. The blood-red forked tongue flicks in the air, tasting it and recognizing potential prey.

It launches off the tree, teeth bared as it lunges for my neck. Instantly I react, as I've done on so many other marsh trips. I hold my spear up in front of me, one hand at either end. The knightcrawler's jaw clamps down on it instead of me. With a practiced motion I flip my spear and fling the knightcrawler to the ground. I dart out of the way of its thrashing claws. It scrambles up and lunges again. This time I grip one end of my spear in both hands and swing hard. It hits the knightcrawler's jaw hard enough to daze it, sending vibrations all the way up my arm. It bites down on the stick in its mouth. For a finishing blow I swing my spear hard against the nearest tree, throwing all my weight into it for leverage. The knightcrawler's head, still clamped on the end, makes a loud cracking sound and leaves a dent in the soft bark of the trunk. My opponent slumps limply to the ground and I wrench my spear out of its mouth.

It isn't dead. I try not to kill these things if I can. I guess it comes from the avoid-violence-at-all-costs mentality that Mistem children are taught from the time they're born. I must have learned something from those lessons. I know the knightcrawlers are just trying to get something to eat and they just happen to be meat-eaters. I'm not going to let myself become a meal for one of them, but whenever possible I try to knock them out instead of killing them. This knightcrawler will wake up soon enough, but I won't be here when it does. Picking up my basket full of berries I turn towards the trail leading home, stowing my spear back in the log as I go, ready for another day's use.

2

The Market

Skylar

When I get home, I find that there was another reason Mom wanted me to go berry picking so early this morning. As I open the door into our small kitchen and the familiar smell of baking wafts toward me, mixed with other cooking smells, I see the rough wooden table laid with all my favourite breakfast foods and my family standing near it waiting for me.

"Happy birthday!" they shout in unison, as if they've been practicing. Mom comes toward me with her mist-grey eyes, common of Mistems, shining with delight. She hugs me as she takes my basket from my hands and puts it on the table.

"The last part we needed for your birthday breakfast," she says with satisfaction. This must have been her idea. She loves to do something special for her family anytime she has an excuse.

"You didn't have to do all this for me!" I'm smiling a bit too much for my protest to be taken seriously. Dad and Mandy just grin.

"Of course we did, it's a special day! And this year is extra special!" Mom's right about that. Today I turn 18, the age when people are officially considered to be adults and are allowed to do a lot of things children can't do. For most people this usually means getting married, but I don't think that's a likely possibility for me. Even though most boys consider me to be pretty, they don't want to spend more time with me than they have to. I don't keep quiet about my opinions and most Mistems think they can be dangerous. Even when boys have tried to court me, I've scared them off in less than a month. Mandy is a different story; she acts more like a "proper" Mistem girl. But I might have ruined her prospects for marriage, too. She's been an adult for two years already, but no one has shown any real interest in her yet. No one wants me for a sister-in-law. I sometimes feel bad about it. I know Mandy wants to get married someday, and even though I don't like any of the boys in our village, I want her to be happy. Still, I just can't seem to keep quiet.

"Enough talking, let's eat! There's a lot of good food here and it's getting cold." Dad is licking his lips and staring hungrily at the spread on the table. I chuckle and sit down.

After we finish eating, Dad pulls out a small package. "For the newest young woman in the family," he says with a flourish. I open it and a small pile of smooth, cool coins falls into my lap. "Now that you're an adult and can make more decisions for yourself, we thought you might like to choose your own gift," he explains when I seem confused. "You can come to the market with me this morning!"

I beam as I thank my family. It must have taken months to save up this money. This is the best gift they could have given me, the opportunity to pick something I really like and a change from the regular routine! Trips into town always tend to be fun for me. We seldom have extra money to spend at the market, so these trips are rare. It's perfect!

* * *

A while later, Dad and I approach the market area in the main village square, a cart laden with berries and baking in tow. I look around the square while helping Dad display our goods and get ready for the day. Everything is the same as it's always been: scattered stands in the middle of the market place where Mistems display and sell their products so that they can feed their families, and Haelton-owned shops in the buildings that surround the square. As in every other part of life in this country, Haelton dominance is made obvious by the way the town is set up.

Soon our stand is ready for business and the first few customers are wandering over. Our customers are often a mixture of Mistems and Haeltons. I can't help but be slightly suspicious as some of the bronze-skinned Haeltons start walking towards us, their golden hair glinting in the sun like the metal it resembles. Usually Mistems and Haeltons don't do business with each other; they try to avoid or ignore each other as much as possible. But sometimes Haeltons go to Mistem stands if they think they can take advantage of how *agreeable* Mistems can be, or if, as in our case, there are no Haelton merchants that sell what we have.

"You can go and do your shopping; I can handle things on my own from here." Dad smiles and waves me away from the stand.

"Dad, do the Haeltons ever try to take advantage of you? You know, try to make you lower the price?" I worry about what happens when other members of my family interact with Haeltons. I can handle any confrontations easily; I stand up for myself. But my family members let the stronger Haeltons walk all over them without putting up a fight, just like other Mistems. They're afraid of every potential problem and avoid conflict at all costs. It's easy for Haeltons to take advantage of them, which is why they've oppressed our race for centuries.

"Don't worry about it, just go and enjoy yourself. I have everything under control here." Somehow, I'm not reassured, but, with a last glance around, I go anyway.

I know exactly where I'm going. I head straight towards the bookstore. When I take a brief look back, Dad is shaking his head as he watches me go. I'm the only Mistem in our village who ever goes into a Haelton-owned shop, and most Mistems don't bother reading for fun anyway. I don't care, though. I love reading, especially exciting stories.

A delightful scent of fresh paper wafts toward me as I open the door and step into a room filled with bookshelves. The shopkeeper, Mark, greets me from behind the counter. "Morning, Misty!" I role my eyes at the nickname. He's called me "Misty" ever since I first walked into his shop. I don't like it, but I gave up trying to correct him when it became apparent that Haeltons somehow find it amusing to watch a Mistem get angry. I head for my favourite section full of adventure stories, which happens to be close to the counter. Shopkeepers are great people to talk to if you want news of the outside world, and the bright-eyed excitement on Mark's face tells me something interesting has happened. I don't have to wait long before he proves me right. "I've heard that the king is returning this week."

"That's great!" I'm momentarily taken away from my browsing. Our village is only an hour's walk away from Vexenta's capital city, Responda. This means that much of our business comes from nobles or their servants who decide that they want to try country stuff for a change. Since most nobles have a habit of following the king when he travels, business slows down a lot when the king isn't home. The newly crowned King Roland has been on a coronation tour to all the major cities in Vexenta, and now he's apparently coming back. Good, business should soon be better. But that isn't all I'm concerned about. "Do you know if he said anything about the war in any of his speeches?"

"Just the usual stuff, as far as I've heard. Thanking the brave warriors, promising victory, saying his age won't hinder anything; all the normal stuff." That doesn't surprise me. Nothing ever really changes when it comes to the war. Vexenta has been at war with our neighbours to the east, Mishfont, for decades. Neither country ever gets any closer to winning, but still, each new king to ascend the throne promises victory during his reign. None of the Mistems believe these speeches, but we never say so and the king doesn't worry about our opinion of anything. No, as long as we keep supporting the war effort by handing over the crops, food, and money we've worked hard for, no one bothers with us. King Roland's speeches aren't meant for the Mistems. He's speaking to the Haeltons, the warriors, the ones who have been taught from birth that fighting shows strength and winning is glory, and to expect each new king to have new strategies that will win the war and make Vexenta an even greater country.

Sure. Keep riding high, Haeltons, on your cloud of grandiose delusions. Pay no attention to the Mistems who support that cloud while remaining firmly grounded in reality. Someday we just might shed this peaceful mindset and let you fall. Of course, I'd never say any of this out loud. I may not be scared to stand up for myself, but I'm not stupid either.

"Why would the king's age be a problem?" I ask, trying to steady my breathing and calm down a little.

"Most people aren't very enthusiastic about entrusting an entire country to an 18-year-old." Yes, like me, the king is just barely an adult. Eight years ago, the former king and queen died in some sort of accident, but King Roland couldn't take the throne until he turned 18.

"I don't see a problem with being 18."

Mark grins at that. "No, I guess you wouldn't. But most people want a king with a bit of experience. They just want to know that King Roland will be as good a ruler as his ancestors." If you could call any of the tyrants who've claimed Vexenta's throne in the past *good*.

I can feel heat rising to my cheeks. I need to get out of this shop. I find a book that looks promising and pay for it, leaving as quickly as I can without betraying the anger that is simmering inside me.

I spend the next few hours simply looking around at the other things for sale in the market. I can almost forget the anger that bubbled up during my conversation with Mark. Almost, until around midday.

I'm walking across the square towards our stand when it happens. A Mistem pushing a heavy cart is coming towards me at the same time as a Haelton is heading to the shop I just left. He's more focused on the store window than anything else. I swerve to avoid the cart, and instead collide with the Haelton. We don't hit each other hard, but he pushes me to the ground in a sudden rage that can only flare up in a Haelton. "Watch where you're going, girl!" The Haeltons in the area glance over without much concern while the Mistems all back away, looking terrified.

The Haelton is waiting for a nervously muttered apology. He expects me to sit in the dirt until he moves on. But I'm not scared; I've done nothing wrong. I stand as quickly as I fell. "I was watching. Maybe you didn't notice the cart, but I did." My tone is matter-of-fact, but the glare I give him is a challenge. I won't back down. Go ahead and start a fight, I'm ready for it. The Mistems are now nowhere to be seen. We're good at hiding; we're taught how to hide from every possible danger from the time we can crawl. Apparently even seeing a conflict arise is dangerous.

It's not surprising that the Haelton takes offense to my unspoken challenge. Haeltons always retaliate when they're offended. This one grabs my arm with bruising strength and pulls me toward him so that our faces are mere inches away. "Watch your attitude, Mistem. It might get you into trouble," he says with a sneer that makes my blood boil.

"Let go of me." My commanding tone only seems to amuse him.

"What if I don't want to?"

Well, I gave him a chance. Besides, he asked a question. It would be rude not to answer him. With a quick twisting motion, I wrench my arm out of his grip and drive my elbow into his jaw. As he stumbles back, too dazed and shocked to react, I pick up my dropped book and stride off toward our stand. Dad is already packing up the goods he didn't get a chance to sell yet.

"Dad, we shouldn't let one bad-tempered Haelton drive us away from the market! We don't have to run away from every little conflict. It doesn't do any good!"

But Dad isn't paying attention to me. True to the ways of the Mistems, he is determined to leave the scene and avoid more trouble. "Let's go," he mutters as he loads the last of the goods onto the cart, disappointment and anger lacing his voice.

* * *

We don't talk on the way back. Dad won't say anything until we get home and he has Mom and Mandy there to back him up.

Mom's questions begin as soon as we open the door. "Why are you home so early? What happened? Are you both all right?"

"We're fine, Mom. There was absolutely no reason for us to come home." I can't keep the annoyance out of my voice, and Mom immediately knows that this is a difference-of-opinion matter. She looks to Dad to explain.

"Skylar got into a fight with a Haelton." My dad glares at me, the blue speckles in his grey eyes almost invisible in our dimly lit house, making them look stormy. He only ever glares when he's really ticked off about something, like if I do something Mistems consider unnecessarily dangerous. I see this look often.

Mom gasps and clasps her hands to her mouth. "Skylar!" she cries, as if begging me to say it isn't true. Mandy's hands freeze midway through kneading pastry dough as she turns to look at me with wide eyes.

"It was not a fight!" I protest. This isn't the first time I've had to make an argument like this, and it will do nothing to help my case, but I continue talking. "A Haelton bumped into me and got angry, and I just showed him he couldn't push me around. It was a disagreement, not a fight."

Dad slams a basket of unsold berries on the table. "You hit him in the face! That's more than a disagreement!"

"He wouldn't let go of my arm, otherwise! Talking wouldn't work, so I used the only thing he would listen to."

"Did you ever consider that he might have hit back? Do you ever think about the consequences your outbursts could have?"

"It's impossible not to when you keep pointing out what *could* happen. Have you ever considered that there might be positive outcomes too? That maybe if we stood up to the Haeltons sometimes they wouldn't treat us like rags?"

"Or that they might get even angrier and make things worse for us? You're too outspoken for your own good, and someday it will get you into serious trouble!"

"How can you know that? You always expect the worst to happen, but it never does! Look, I'm fine, you're fine, and nothing's damaged, so what is there to be afraid of?"

"Skylar," Mom, who until now had been watching the exchange between Dad and I in shocked silence, breaks in with a scared whisper. "We just don't want to see you get hurt."

"And I don't want us to spend our entire lives as puppets to the Haeltons, to be used and abused when they want something from us and completely ignored when they don't. Everyone's too scared to even look them in the eyes! Have you ever considered that things could be different? That we could be equals with the Haeltons? That we might not have to constantly be hiding and running from every little potential problem? I don't want trouble, but I don't want any of us to be treated like scum either." Before anyone can respond, I retreat to the small bedroom Mandy and I share. I flop onto my bed and begin to lose myself in my new book. At least in books there's more excitement than scuffles in the market and oft-repeated family arguments. At least in books every problem has a definite resolution, usually in favour of the hero.

3

Trouble

Skylar

It's decided that I'm not allowed to go to the market until I learn to control my impulsiveness. Dad calls it "protecting me from myself"; I call it being paranoid. For the rest of the week I'm confined to the regular routine around the house. This mostly involves helping Mom and Mandy with the baking and housework when they need an extra hand. I'm glad I still have my book and berry picking to turn to for excitement.

This morning I'm in the marshes again. It's bright and sunny, a perfect day for berry picking. As I hunt for berries, navigating through the mucky ground near the road, I come across a cluster of trees that are heavily laden with bunches of the juicy delicacy. I grin and look around at the dangling fruit all around me, swaying in the breeze above my head. This should be fun! Placing my basket on the ground I immediately begin my gathering.

I climb part way up the trees then launch off them, spinning and flipping in the air sometimes, leaving little time between every throw of my spear. I don't stop to put the berries in my basket yet, instead letting them fall to the ground. I laugh with delight as I fly from tree to tree, my collection of fallen fruit growing with each passing minute. Sadly, though, good times tend to end, and soon there is little fruit left in the trees. With one last jump and throw I down a few more arda berries and flip in the air before landing in a crouch and standing quickly, my arms flung up in triumph. I retrieve my spear from where it landed and begin putting the fallen berries into my basket.

As I gather my bounty, still grinning, I hear a sound I never expected. Someone is applauding!

Clutching my spear, I whip around to face my audience. It's a Haelton, but not just any Haelton. He's wearing a formal military uniform with a purple cape draping almost to the ground. In the dappled light beneath the trees, a gold signet ring, the kind nobles wear, glints dully on the middle finger of his right hand. On his head is a crown, like a wreath of golden swords with blood-red rubies in the hilts, all of them pointing upwards. Behind him, on the road, an elaborate carriage waits with two guards standing at attention near it. Both the carriage and the guards' uniforms have a coat of arms on them, two swords crossed behind a crown much like the one worn by the Haelton. My berry-picking performance is being applauded by King Roland of Vexenta!

I dip into a quick curtsey, though I probably look awkward doing it, and wait for the king to either speak or leave. He stops clapping and puts one hand on the ornate hilt of a sword at his side, his eyes rapidly darting around the marshes. Then he chooses to speak.

"That was quite an impressive display, My Lady."

My Lady?! Is he blind? What Mistem would ever be a noble? I decide to be polite and pretend to be a normal Mistem, though. Maybe he'll get bored and leave me alone. "Thank you, Your Majesty," I say, trying to put a nervous quaver in my voice. "But, Sire, I am not a noblewoman. I'm just a simple Mistem."

The king smiles. "I know that you are a Mistem, but you are certainly not simple." He looks around in an exaggerated, thoughtful way, then smirks. "This is not a place where any normal Mistem would ever come, is it?" I slowly shake my head, then pretend to look at the ground, watching the king from under my lashes. He studies me. "Someone brave enough to come here alone could fit quite well as a member of my court."

"Thank you, Your Majesty. I'm flattered," I say, trying to hide the fact that my teeth are grinding. The king might think that calling me a lady is a compliment, but I don't take it that way. I never want to be associated in any way with those pompous, self-centered jerks.

The king's gaze sweeps around the trees again, his hand tight on his sword, before it fixes on me. His eyes, a bright yellow-gold like the sun, are staring intently as they slide from my face, all the way down my body, and back again. It makes me uncomfortable. I'm relieved when he goes to examine my berry collection.

"Is this a habit of yours? Coming to the marshes?"

Is he just trying to make small talk, or is he trying to find something out? It might not be safe to answer honestly, but he definitely won't believe this is my first time here after what he saw. I settle for a half-truth. "I come once in a while."

"What's the reason for it?"

"I'm sorry?"

"There must be a reason for someone to be in a place such as this. Why do you keep coming here?"

"For the arda berries, Sire."

"Is that the only reason?"

What's he trying to get at? "Yes, Your Majesty."

"Don't the creatures here give you trouble when you come?"

"Not really." That's true enough; they just add more excitement to my routine.

"The beasts never attack you?" he raises an eyebrow.

"I simply leave if I see any."

He gazes at me intently, folding one arm over his chest and scratching his chin with the other, before speaking again. "Tell me, My Lady, do you think I'm foolish?"

Yes, but this time I'm sure honesty would get me arrested. "Of course not, Sire."

"Do you think I can't tell when someone is pretending to be something they aren't?"

Is my acting that bad? I decide to play dumb, though. "I don't know what you mean, Sire."

He's pacing around me, his hand back on the sword hilt, constantly looking between me and the fallen berries.

"Come, stop this nonsense. An average Mistem would ever come near a place like this. What is your true reason for being here?"

It's a relief to stop acting scared. I never want to cower in front of anyone, especially Haeltons. I draw myself up to my full height and stare straight into his golden-yellow eyes. "I don't think my motivations are any of your concern."

I expect the king to be angry that I'm refusing to answer him, but he's not. Instead he smiles as if he's won some sort of competition. "Shouldn't a ruler care about the lives of his subjects?"

"You've never cared about us before." I put as much venom into my voice as I can.

"Perhaps I want to change things."

"I doubt it."

The king smiles as if he's amused by my outspokenness. He becomes quiet, staring with his head tilted to one side as if he's studying me. Soon he makes a decision. "It seems a waste that a girl as unique as yourself should be confined to a place such as this. Perhaps you would like to accompany me back to my palace. You can be my guest there."

Guest. Whatever he means by that, I don't like the sound of it. I feign politeness, even as an angry flush creeps onto my face at what he's suggesting. "Thank you for the offer, but I'm afraid I can't accept. I must return to my family today."

"I'm certain that your family will be fine without you."

"They'll be worried if I don't return before nightfall."

"They will know soon enough what has become of you."

He's determined to get me to go with him. I give up all pretense of politeness and use the most commanding tone I can muster. "I'm not going with you. I'm returning home—today."

I'm tempted to slap the king and wipe the condescending smirk off his face. But he glances over my shoulder and nods, and before I can raise a hand to hit him, strong hands seize my wrists from either side. I was so focused on my conversation with the king that I didn't notice his guards sneaking towards us until they jump at me from behind the trees. I can easily take on one Haelton in the market, but when two well-trained palace guards take me by surprise? The king doesn't seem to believe in a fair fight. I could almost laugh at the irony. He's supposed to be a strong, feared war leader, yet he needs to call in reinforcements to handle a single Mistem girl. Tough warrior, riiiiiiight. The guard on my right wrenches my spear from my grasp and throws it on the ground beside my basket. Great. Now I'm trapped and weaponless with the Haelton king leering at me.

"It appears we have competing intentions, then. But tell me, My Lady, in a battle of wills, who do you think would win?" He leans forward and whispers in my ear. His next words make my skin crawl, "I always get what I want."

He turns away and heads toward his carriage, and I have no choice but to follow as his goons drag me along. My mind races as I try to find ways to escape, but I can't shake the guards holding me prisoner.

When we get to the carriage the king offers me his hand to help me get into it. As if chivalry will make things better. I ignore his hand and climb in on my own. The creep chuckles! He won't stop looking at me as he takes the velvet-covered seat across from me, but I absolutely refuse to meet his eyes. I stare out the window instead as the carriage begins to move. I can only settle in for what will probably be the longest and worst journey of my life.

4

The King

Roland

When I left the palace to deal with the cowards trying to stir up trouble in my absence, I expected only headaches and frustration. Why must they try to turn the country against me in the first two months of my reign? Must I make an example of my own subjects already?

Then, however, I found a jewel.

The Mistem sitting across from me refuses to look away from the window, so I point out features of the landscape. She remains stonily silent and gives no indication that she hears me.

"Have you ever left your village before?" I ask, trying to engage her in conversation.

The only response she gives is the slightest shake of her head. The white strands of hair which escaped her braid during her spectacular performance in the marsh sway with the motion. They catch the light from the window, giving the appearance of stars framing her moon-pale face.

"Where did you learn to use that staff of yours so well?" I try again.

Nothing.

I want to ask how she can stand to set foot in those marshes alone and almost unarmed, but that would suggest I fear doing the same. I will never admit that to anyone. Normally I cannot even look at the marshes when the carriage drives past them. When I heard laughter among the trees and ordered the driver to stop, only the knowledge that my guards were watching could make me walk close enough to investigate.

So what gives a Mistem girl such courage?

Though she's scowling and refuses to talk now, I will find out soon. I will show her the best time at tonight's party and convince her to forgive me for the rather aggressive invitation I gave.

First, though, I must take her attention away from the window.

"How long have you been going to the marshes?"

Still nothing.

"What need do you have for so many berries?"

The Mistem may as well be a statue.

Now my patience wanes.

"Have you suddenly lost your ability to speak?" I ask with a mocking smile.

Silence.

"Most people would respond when questioned by royalty." My annoyance starts to show in my voice, despite my constant attempts to seem calm and in control.

Now the Mistem speaks for the first time since we got into the carriage. "I have nothing to say."

It isn't much, but it's something. "Perhaps you can answer a simple question, then. What is your name?" Only now do I realize that I never asked her name. She may have had a point when she said I care little about commoners.

When she responds, her voice is so low that I almost miss the single word she utters, "Skylar."

"It suits you. Beautiful and unique. It stands out as you do."

She scoffs at that. "You say that as if standing out is a good thing."

"It is in your case. You're like a gorgeous rose, blossoming in a garden full of daisies."

She does not respond to my poetic compliment the way I thought she would. She smirks, as if I said something funny. "Roses have thorns, Your Majesty. Most people don't want to get too close to them."

It's my turn to smirk. "I can handle a few sharp points, Rose Blossom."

She finally looks at me. No, she glares at me. Her eyes briefly meet mine, blazing with fury, before she turns back to the window, scowling at the scenery. I don't think she likes the nickname.

We've come to the outskirts of Respenda. As we enter the city, Skylar sinks back in her seat. She can still see out the window, but no one looking into the carriage would notice her. "What's wrong?" I ask jokingly. "You don't want to be seen in a big city?"

"Not with you."

Ouch. A grimacing half-smile crosses my face. "You may have been correct about the thorns," I mutter.

Skylar doesn't respond, but a triumphant glint appears in her eyes as she suppresses the smile playing on her lips.

I know my subjects in the city are pausing to watch the carriage go by—as they always do—but I don't look at them. I wave nonchalantly and continue to watch the Mistem seated across from me. Her eyes dart back and forth as she takes in the sights of the city.

"I imagine this is quite different from your hometown."

She shakes her head. "The only difference I see is the amount of people."

Confused, I glance out the window at the passing buildings. I don't usually go into small country villages like the one she probably lives in, but I pass by them sometimes, close enough to see what's there. The mansions and public buildings here are far more impressive than the ramshackle housing and shops that make up those villages. What could she mean?

Glancing back at Skylar, it's apparent that she isn't looking at the buildings. Her eyes are pointed downwards. I turn back, looking down at the street this time. It is filled with the usual crowd of people going about their daily business, pausing to look up at my carriage and respectfully bow or curtsey as we pass. Wait, it's only Haeltons who look up at me. The few Mistems that can be seen keep their heads down, staring at the ground. I'm surprised at how few of them I see; I thought there were more of them in this city. Then I notice the white heads darting through the crowds, often ducking out of view. They're so easy to overlook, almost invisible if you don't actively search for them.

I glance over at Skylar again, sitting across from me, though no one we pass ever seems to notice her. She's invisible to the people of the city because she doesn't want to be seen. However, she was noticeable enough just a few minutes earlier. Do Mistems usually choose to remain inconspicuous, or are they so used to being invisible that they disappear without realizing it? Skylar was correct when she stated that I never noticed Mistems before, but can she hold me accountable for that when they're often so hard to spot?

I watch for Skylar's reaction as the carriage pulls up to the doors of the palace. She doesn't seem to react much, though I notice that her eyes are intensely focused, as if she's trying to memorize every detail. Perhaps she's impressed. When the carriage stops, I exit first and again offer my hand to my Mistem guest. "Shall we, Rose?" She glowers at me and avoids my hand as if it's diseased. Flanked by guards we enter the palace, Skylar's eyes still roaming over everything. Sadly, I can't give her a tour myself, since I still have preparations to oversee for the party, so I give instructions to one of the guards, who nods and escorts her away. She doesn't even glance at me as she follows him. She simply holds her head high and walks away with all the defiance and dignity of a captured princess in the heart of enemy territory.

5

Palace Life

Skylar

T he guard leads me down a hall with paintings of past kings and queens. He steers me to the right at the end of it. Then a left turn. Right again. Left, right, left, left down the third hallway branching off the corridor of windows overlooking a fountain. Or was it the second? It's impossible to remember the way out of this labyrinthine palace. It's huge, and every inch of it is elaborately decorated. We turn right into a hall lined with suits of armour, most of them made of bronze.

"Enjoying the artwork?" the guard asks nonchalantly, noting my gaze. I don't respond, but he continues talking. "These suits are only meant for decoration. The armour used in battle is usually made of steel overlaid with bronze, to make it stronger while giving a visual statement." Typical Haeltons. They always have to draw attention to themselves and show off.

We reach a hallway with doors all along both sides. It must be a guest area or something. The sounds of activity drift from behind the doors, though no one is in the hall at the moment. The guard leads me to a door at the end of the hall and bows as he opens it, waving me in. As the door closes behind me, my eyes sweep the room. It, like everything else in the palace, is meant to show off. This one room is bigger than my house! The furniture is covered in decorative carving, the bed and couches piled with soft cushions made from silky fabrics, and the walls are draped with tapestries. Does the king think this will impress me? Because all I can think is that if Haeltons have this much money, why do they need to take anything from Mistems to support the war?

I walk over to one of the large windows that flood the room with sunlight. All that's visible is a courtyard surrounded by other parts of the palace, but it gives me an idea. Don't palaces usually have gardens or lawns or some sort of open area? There might be fewer guards in a spot like that. Maybe I could convince the king to take me for a walk in the gardens, and then kick him and run. Mistems are as good at running as we are at hiding. I could easily get away before any Haelton guards could possibly catch up.

The sound of the door opening again distracts me from my scheming. I spin, expecting to see King Roland, but no, it's a Mistem. A maid, I realize, as I notice her uniform. Could she have been one of the king's previous *guests*? Will I face the same fate of palace servitude if I don't escape? The maid hasn't noticed me yet, and I watch as she makes her way toward the bed, eyes fixed on the floor, a bundle of fabric in her arms. Finally, she looks up at me and nearly drops her load.

"I—I apologize, My Lady," she stammers, quickly recovering from the shock. "I was just surprised. W-We've never had a Mistem stay here before, as far as I can recall." So, I'm the first Mistem guest. I don't know if that's a good thing.

"Don't worry, you don't need to apologize," I say, trying to calm down the maid.

"Thank you, My Lady," she replies with a curtsey. I see we need to set some things straight.

"Please don't call me 'My Lady'. I'm not a noblewoman."

"If that is what My Lady wishes, I will stop."

Sigh. "Please, just call me 'Skylar.'"

"Of course, Miss Skylar." Good enough.

"What's your name?" She pauses in her task of spreading out the fabric she brought, which I now realize is an extravagant gown, and stares into the distance with wide eyes. It seems she isn't asked this question very often.

"My name isn't important, Miss."

"Neither was mine until about an hour ago. But I want to know your name." I give her a kind, encouraging smile. It's time Mistems stopped seeing themselves as unimportant.

She smiles shyly and answers, "Ann".

"And no one told you there was a Mistem in this room, Ann?"

"All I was told was that there was a new guest in this room, and I was supposed to help you get ready." She holds up the gown for me to see. It's purple with silver embroidery around the neck, hem, and cuffs. It's beautiful, flowy, and elegant. It's old, though. The color has faded slightly and the silver threads have sunken into the fabric in some places and are coming loose in others. It's likely an extra gown they had in storage; it might even be one of the old queen's gowns. There are undergarments too, corsets and things to make the skirt of the dress puff out. "Shall I help you?" Ann asks.

"No, thank you. I'd rather get dressed in private." Ann doesn't argue, and I gather up the garments and take them into the bathroom that's attached to the bedroom. Hiding the undergarments behind the ornate bathtub, I proceed to put the gown on over my work clothes. If I get a chance to escape, I don't want my family questioning me about my attire. It's a good thing the gown has long sleeves and a high neckline, so no one can see what's underneath.

When I step out of the bathroom, Ann ushers me into a chair in front of a dressing table and mirror. She undoes my braid and lays the string I had tied to the end of it on the table. I quickly grab it before she can notice and tie it onto my arm. Then I get an idea. "Ann, does the palace have a garden?"

"Yes, Miss. Just past the buildings on the other side of the courtyard." Suddenly she frowns in suspicion. "Why do you ask?"

I'm sure she would never dare to question my motives if I were a Haelton noblewoman, but she's gotten a bit bolder as we've been talking. I don't mind, but it still probably isn't a good idea to trust her with my escape plans. "I come from a country village. I like being outside."

She nods sympathetically. "I understand, Miss, though I'm afraid you might not be able to visit the gardens today."

"Why not?"

"Because of the party."

"Party? What party?" My question brings a startled look to Ann's wide eyes, and she launches into a quick explanation.

"There is a party today to celebrate the king's return. I was told that you are to attend, and that is what I'm getting you ready for." As an afterthought she mumbles an apology, "I thought you knew."

So, the king wants to parade me around in front of a bunch of Haelton nobles at his party like some sort of exotic accessory? Or worse, a circus freak? An image of the king creeps into my mind, walking with me into a ballroom, a self-satisfied grin on his face. *"Look at what I found! A brave Mistem! You'll never guess what she was doing when I saw her!"* My fists clench, crumpling the skirt of the costume I've been forced to wear.

It truly is a costume. When Ann finishes, and I stand in front of a full-length mirror to inspect her work, I don't recognise myself. The bodice of the dress is gathered in at the waist and the sleeves are tight-fitting up to my elbows, then both skirt and sleeves flare out to flow gracefully around me. My hair is now in a complicated bun with amethysts braided into it. And when I thought Ann was just taking the dirt off my face from my berry-picking excursion, she was also putting make-up on me. I've never worn make-up before, but now my eyelids are purple, to match the dress, blush makes my pale cheekbones stand out, and my lips have gone from being light pink to subtle red. The country girl I'm familiar with is gone, replaced by someone who could almost pass for nobility. I cringe at the thought.

When the door opens again, King Roland walks in. Ann curtseys quickly and scurries out, eyes fixed on the floor once again. The king doesn't even glance at her; his eyes are fixed on me. He grins as he looks me over. "Don't you look stunning, Rose!"

I glare at him, my arms crossed over my chest. "I have a name, you know."

"Yes, of course, but the nickname suits you so well." Is he purposely trying to antagonise me for his own amusement?

"You didn't say there was a party you wanted me to attend." My annoyance is clear in my voice, and I make no attempt to hide it.

"Did I forget to mention that? I apologize, I'm afraid I was distracted. But, seeing as you know now, shall we make our way down?" He holds out his arm for me to take. As if I'm going to act like a willing accessory.

"I wonder if you ever considered that I might not want to attend, Your Majesty?"

He raises his eyebrows, as if such a concept is unthinkable. "I've never known anyone who wouldn't enjoy an event such as this."

I mutter my response as I push past him into the hall, "As we've established, I'm not like other people."

A sudden idea occurs to me as I reach the door. What would happen if I just kept going? Maybe I could get away before anyone could catch me. But then I hesitate, noticing the guards placed on either side of the door. I'm truly a prisoner here.

In my moment of hesitation, the king catches up to me, and I see a smirk playing on his lips. I keep walking, staring straight ahead and remaining silent as he falls into step beside me. He doesn't try to make me talk this time, and so I'm left in peace as I once again attempt to memorize the maze of a route I'm led through.

I expect to be taken into some sort of ballroom crowded with Haeltons in fancy clothes. Instead, the king takes me to a highly decorated set of double doors which seem to lead outside. My heart beats faster in excitement. If the party is taking place on open ground outside, I might be able to make a break for it. However, when the doors are opened, I don't see steps leading down onto the ground. The doors lead onto a balcony overlooking . . . . A stadium? An arena? It's a circular, roofless building, with seats at different levels all the way up the sides. The seats are crowded with Haeltons in fancy clothes, but the balcony I stand on with the king is empty except for the two of us, two seats, and some sort of large gong. In the center of the structure is a sandy floor. Two Haeltons stand in the middle of it, each clutching a long, wooden staff.

"What's this?" I ask, curiosity momentarily taking over my rebellious inclinations.

The king smiles vaguely, as if it's supposed to be some sort of surprise. "It's a bit of, shall we say, entertainment before the party." I look again at the Haeltons in the middle of the arena. It looks like they're going to fight each other. Of course, a Haelton's idea of entertainment would involve some form of violence.

I sit down in one of the seats on the balcony, placed close enough to the railing that I have a good view of everything in the arena. Since I obviously won't be able to get away until this *entertainment* is over, I'll just have to wait it out.

King Roland steps forward and begins speaking, his voice carrying through the whole arena. "The men you see before you are traitors to their nation and their race. They are cowards who refuse to fight for the glory of our noble country and would rather incite opposition to our war effort." I'm starting to like those two Haeltons better than anyone I see in the seats. What the king says next, though, makes the blood drain from my face.

"These men have committed terrible crimes against their country, but they have a chance to redeem themselves. If they can prove themselves to be worthy warriors against some of our land's most dangerous creatures, their lives will be spared. They must either prove their strength or die in the attempt." I look again at the men in the middle of the arena. They are both wearing plain clothes, not armour. And their only weapons are big sticks. I doubt even the best Haelton warriors would go up against whatever beasts are about to be released on these two without being better armed. This isn't a competition; this isn't a fair chance. This is an execution.

I get up and walk to where King Roland is standing, getting ready to strike the gong that will signal the death of these men. "Your Majesty?" He pauses and turns to me, then nods for me to continue speaking. "I'm just wondering if these men got a fair trial before they were sent into the arena."

He scoffs. "There was no need. These men are traitors, plain and simple, and they needed to be dealt with quickly."

"Were they gaining followers? Were they really starting a serious rebellion?"

"Not yet, they were caught before they could make much progress. But it's good to deal with these things before they become a problem."

"So, basically, they're being executed for stating their opinions."

"They have a chance to save themselves." He scowls at my obvious disapproval. Perhaps I should be careful, before he labels me a traitor and a rebel, but my conscience won't let me sit by idly and let innocent men die.

"What chance?! You give them a stick to fend off deadly monsters and call that fair? That's as good as murder!" My voice is rising, and the Haeltons are starting to look this way. I don't care. Maybe it's time someone pointed out to them how stupid their war obsession is.

"Sit down!" the king commands. I stand my ground.

"Not when lives are on the line."

He glares and turns away, getting ready to strike the gong. I can't just let that happen. Lunging forward I grab his arm, trying to pull him away. His face flushes a coppery-red in anger.

"I SAID, 'SIT DOWN'!" He tries to shake me off, but I hold firm.

"NO! I WON'T JUST SIT HERE AND LET YOU KILL INNOCENT PEOPLE, YOU TYRANT!"

The look on the king's face turns from overt rage to something colder, and somehow more deadly. I know I've gone too far, but it's too late to take back what I said. Grabbing my arm, he snarls into my face, "Then you can join them!" The next second, he hurls me over the edge of the balcony.

6

The Arena

Skylar

It's dark. Did I black out? I wouldn't be surprised if I did; that was a 15 or 20-foot fall, and I didn't land too well. I couldn't have been unconscious for more than a moment, though, because when I open my eyes, most people in the arena seats are still trying to figure out what happened. I can see the Haeltons closest to me. Some look bored, but others have pity written on their faces. Funny, I thought they would be jeering at the Mistem who was stupid enough to yell at the king. The two Haeltons I was yelling for are bending over me, looks of amazement and hopelessness on their faces.

"Thank you for trying to help us, Mistem," says the one in the faded blue shirt.

His counterpart, wearing a brown shirt, nods in agreement and adds, "It looks like it was all for nothing, though. We're still doomed."

These two are supposed to be from the warrior race, so why am I the one who still has a will to fight? I stand quickly, though it makes my head swim, and the Haeltons stand too. "We're not doomed unless we give up. If they want to see a fight, let's give them one."

A glint in the sand catches my eye. I run over to see what it is. It's a long, heavy chain, possibly used to lock up my Haelton friends before they were brought here. Perfect; now we all have some sort of weapon. As I pick it up, the sound of the gong rings out over the arena. Wait, the king didn't ring it before? Why did he hesitate? But I have no time to figure out the answer, and I quickly run back to the Haeltons. It will be easier to fight whatever's being released on us if we fight together.

The sound of metal scraping on metal draws my attention to the gate of iron bars opening on the other side of the arena. I laugh aloud in relief and triumph as our opponents exit their cage; knightcrawlers. And there's only two of them. This will be easier than I thought. The Haeltons beside me stare, as if I've lost my mind, and back away from me. Still smiling I turn to them. "Don't worry, we can get out of this. Could either of you use this as a weapon?" I hold up the chain. Apparently, they both think it's a better option than the staffs, because they immediately grab for it. Blue Shirt gets it first, and I take his staff. Now this is a fair fight.

No sooner am I armed and ready, than the knightcrawlers have reached us. The Haeltons back away, but I aim the end of my staff at the first knightcrawler and ram it between its eyes. It isn't knocked out, but it's dazed. The Haeltons are encouraged by my success and both begin to take on the other knightcrawler.

I don't know how long the fight lasts. I don't hear the reactions of the crowd and I barely notice what happens in the fight between the two Haeltons and the other knightcrawler. I only focus on my own opponent, and it's almost like I'm back in the marsh and this is just another day of berry picking. It lunges at me and I duck, jamming my staff under its chin. It falls and scrambles for my feet. I jump, landing hard with my feet planted on its back before stepping off to the side. At last the knightcrawler half gets up and I manage to ram my stick onto its chest. The creature falls backwards and whacks its head against one of the arena walls. It slumps to the ground. I stand looking at it, enjoying my victory and catching my breath.

Then I'm reminded that I'm not at home. Dagger-sharp claws seize my arm from behind. I grasp my staff, getting ready to turn on the other attacker, but Blue Shirt beats me to it. He wraps his chain around the knightcrawler's neck while it's focused on me and yanks it back. I barely notice as the claws rip through the sleeves of both my garments and tear the skin beneath. Instead I watch as Blue Shirt pulls the knightcrawler to the ground and Brown Shirt delivers a finishing blow to its head with his staff.

The crowd erupts. We've won, but somehow, I doubt the king will set us free. I don't trust the promises he made for show. "Let's go! This way!" I shout to my celebrating arena comrades. I think we share the same distrust of the king, because they follow me without question. We run toward the gate that the knightcrawlers came through, kicking up a cloud of dust behind us. It's a way out of the arena, and we can probably slip through the bars.

We reach the gate just as the king's voice rings out over the noise of the crowd. "After them!" he yells from his throne above the arena. We need to move quickly. I slip easily through the bars. I'm thin like other Mistems; no bars built to hold back brawny, thick-skinned monsters would hold me back. The Haeltons have a bit more trouble getting through, but they manage and soon we're rushing along the dim, cool tunnels beneath the arena. There must be a way out through them, otherwise how would they have gotten the knightcrawlers in here?

I have to hold up the skirt of the gown that's on me, so I don't trip, but it makes running awkward. Why does anyone wear these things? The pounding of the Haeltons' feet and their panting breath echoes off the walls as we weave through the tunnels. Soon I see light coming from a side passage and I bolt towards it, the Haeltons struggling to keep up. Yes, it's another gate. This one leads to open ground, outside the palace walls. The looming trees of a forest are nearby. Perfect. In a matter of moments, we're through the gate and running toward the forest. I grab the hands of the Haeltons and pull them along behind me, slowing my pace a bit so they don't stumble over their own feet. I can't go very fast anyway, in this dress. I keep stepping on the hem, though the sound of it tearing is drowned out by the blood rushing in my ears and the panting of my companions.

We reach the edge of the forest just as guards burst from the arena doors. We run in, careful not to break any sticks and leave a trail that they could follow. Suddenly I stop. "Quick! Climb up this tree!" I tell the Haeltons, pointing to a tall tree with some low branches.

"Are you crazy?" asks Brown Shirt. "You want to make it easy for them to catch us?!"

"Trust me!" I don't have time to explain, and they don't have a better option, so we hoist ourselves up and climb as high as we dare. I remember being taught as a kid to always climb if I'm trying to hide from a person. Unless they're looking for birds, people never look up.

We wait, not moving at all, hardly daring to breath. And soon they come, crashing through the forest, looking all around them, but never looking up. It works—they don't see us! And after a few minutes the guards move on, oblivious to our presence. Sometimes it's good to be easily overlooked.

We wait until the sound of the guards marching through the forest has long faded into the distance and we're sure no one is around to hear us. Then we climb down and begin talking in low voices. "I can't believe that worked!" Blue Shirt whispers.

"Never doubt a Mistem when it comes to hiding," I reply simply.

"Now what do we do?" asks Brown Shirt, his expression changing from triumphant excitement to fearful concern.

"We should probably get out of here. I doubt the king will keep his promise to let you two go free, and he never promised me anything." The Haeltons nod their agreement.

"It wouldn't be easy to leave the country, but if we can get far enough away, to a village near the border, we should be safe." Brown Shirt suggests.

"Then you two should get going now, so you can get a head start."

"You should come with us, Mistem. You're not safe staying here either."

I shake my head. "I have a family here. I can't just leave them. Besides, the government doesn't keep track of where Mistems live. I should be safe enough there."

The Haeltons stare at me in concern, but they don't argue. Blue Shirt just shakes his head and says, "I can't tell if you're extremely brave, or extremely stupid, Mistem."

I smile a little. Then Brown Shirt speaks. "I never thought I'd say this to a Mistem, but you just saved our lives. I don't know how we could ever thank you enough."

"Just make sure the effort wasn't in vain." With that we part ways, and I begin to shed my palace costume.

My hair is soon back in its usual plain braid, the makeup is rubbed off, and I begin to take off the gown. I wince as I pull off the right sleeve and a stinging sensation shoots through my arm. Now I notice the wound from the knightcrawler for the first time. The sleeves of both my work clothes and the palace dress are torn and blood-soaked. On my arm, just above the elbow, are three long, deep gashes. When I first started berry picking, I would get hurt in fights with knightcrawlers on a regular basis, but this wound is worse than anything I ever got before. It's going to be hard to explain this. I look up at the sky. It's been hours since the king first saw me in the marshes and the sun is starting to set. Maybe it will be dark enough by the time I get home that I can keep my family from noticing I'm hurt and hide all evidence of it by morning. Then all I have to do is find a way to explain my long absence. I won't tell them the true story. They can't do anything about it, so there's no point in causing them to worry. Besides, this is my fight, just my will versus the king's; they don't need to get involved.

With a myriad of possible excuses rushing through my mind, and most of the evidence from my excursion to the palace lying on the forest floor, I head home into the gathering darkness. I keep to the shadows as much as possible, listening intently for any sign that I'm being followed.

7

The Aftermath

Roland

I'm completely still, hunched over the balcony railing, my eyes refusing to focus on anything, as the nobility file out toward the ballroom. I can't make it seem like this incident bothered me by cancelling the party. Still, the thought of facing their questions is abhorrent.

I lost control. I threw Skylar into the arena in the heat of the moment, purely out of anger and frustration. I immediately regretted it, but could I take back that decision in front of everyone? No, people doubt me enough already. All I could do was wait to have the knightcrawlers released until she had a weapon.

This girl keeps surprising me. Does Skylar have absolutely no fear at all? She may have screamed while falling, but her reaction to the knight-crawlers shocked everyone in the audience. She laughed! She actually laughed! Either she hit her head on the way down, or she's a braver war-rior than half the people in my court. After watching her fight, I believe it's the latter.

"Sire?" My musings are interrupted by the captain of the guard. He's standing too still and straight, posturing the way he does when he's ner-vous, and staring at a point just past my head. I don't expect him to have good news.

"Have you found them?" My voice is hard and angry, and the captain steps back slightly. I know the answer before he says it.

"No, Sire. There was no sign of them. All we found was this." He holds up a purple gown, the one Skylar was wearing. It's now dirty, torn, and stained with blood. It briefly brings back memories of the person for whom it was made. I quickly suppress those thoughts as the captain speaks again. "Shall we continue looking for the convicts, Sire?"

I pause. "No. I said they would be spared if they survived in the arena, and I'll keep my word. Let them go and focus on finding the Mistem girl."

"Sire, we have no idea where she might have gone."

"She was in the marshes when I saw her. Send spies to all the villages in that area. Bring her here when she's found."

"Yes, Your Majesty." He leaves quickly.

My mind is constantly on Skylar as I walk towards the ball room. I suppose I'm not the only one thinking about her. I expect to receive a lot of questions today about the mysterious Mistem. At least it's something new to talk about, and the conversations won't all be about war and politics. That can be sickeningly dull sometimes. I reach the ballroom door and brace myself. Taking a breath and holding my head high, I enter, and the party begins.

8

Home Again

Skylar

It's dark when I arrive home. My family usually isn't awake for very long after sunset, but there's light coming through the kitchen window. They must be waiting for me. Apparently, they've been waiting by the windows, because I'm still a good distance away when the door bursts open and my family comes rushing towards me. Mom reaches me first, and I turn my uninjured side to her as she embraces me, returning her hug with my good arm.

"Oh, Skylar, we're so glad you're safe! We were so worried! We thought you'd gotten hurt!"

"I'm fine, Mom."

Dad and Mandy soon catch up. They don't say anything at first, but their faces have broken into relieved smiles. "Let's go inside," Dad says as he puts an arm around me and guides me toward the house.

"We've got supper waiting. I'll go get you some." Mandy runs into the house ahead of us. I'm glad we only have a single lantern to light our house at night. It's dark enough that no one has noticed my injured arm yet. Maybe I can get away with this.

As I sit down in the kitchen and Mandy hands me some soup and bread, I suddenly feel as if I'm on trial. When Dad speaks, it's clear that I am. "Where were you? Why didn't you come home?"

"I was in the berry patch, and I heard a noise. It sounded like something was coming right at me. I ran away. But when I stopped, I didn't recognise where I was. I hadn't gone that far before. It took me a long time to find my way back."

"What was coming at you?"

"I don't know. I didn't look."

Dad raises an eyebrow. "And you didn't pay attention to where you were going?"

"No, not really. I was more focused on getting out of danger," I shrug.

"When you didn't even know if you were in danger? When you didn't know what was making the sound? You?" Mom and Dad exchange a glance as Mandy looks at me with half-closed eyed. I didn't expect anyone to believe me, but that was the plan. Now if I tell them a slightly more believable story, one that might get me into a little bit of trouble, they'll be more likely to believe it because it looked like I was trying to hide it.

"Well, okay, I–"

Dad cuts me off. "Before you start telling another story, why don't you explain this." To my horror, he puts my berry basket on the table, along with my spear.

"Where did you–? How–?"

Mandy answers the questions I can't seem to finish. "When you didn't come back by the middle of the afternoon, we went looking for you. We couldn't find any sign of you anywhere. We didn't know where else to look, so I went to the outskirts of the marshes and searched around there. I saw something in the trees that looked weird, and when I went closer to investigate, I found these surrounded by fallen berries."

I stare at her. She actually went into the marshes? Either Mandy's braver than I give her credit for, or they really were desperate to find me. Dad doesn't give me time to think about this. "Care to explain?"

Maybe I can use this to my advantage. I can distract them with a little truth. I take a breath and answer, "Arda berries grow best in the marshes."

Their reaction is like an explosion.

"You've been going there this whole time?"

"What were you thinking?"

"Don't you know what kinds of creatures live in that place?"

"Yes, I know, I know." I point to my spear. "I was careful and ready in case anything dangerous came after me."

"Ready to do what, exactly?" Dad asks, looking at the stick on the table with narrowed eyes. "If you thought you could fight those things . . . ."

They aren't ready to hear the full truth. "I left if I saw any creatures. The spear was just a precaution in case I couldn't get away. I mostly use it to get berries out of the trees."

"And what happened today? Why were these abandoned, and why were you gone for so long?"

Now for a more believable story. "I got lost running from a knightcrawler."

"WHAT?! Don't you know how dangerous knightcrawlers are? Haven't we taught you anything? How could you think that was a good idea?"

"Dad, I'm fine! I know exactly what they can do, and that's why I have the spear and I make sure I can get away from them! You always talk about the bad things that *could* happen, but—" I'm about to say *but they never do* when Mom's horrified gasp stops me. I had been gesturing to emphasize my point. Bad idea. My blood-soaked sleeve caught the light from the lantern. Dad reaches for my arm to look at it, but I pull it away. "I climbed a tree to get away and got cut on a branch." It's the same kind of excuse I would always use years ago when I got hurt. I hope it works again. "It's nothing."

"Then why is there so much blood on your sleeve?"

"Because I was walking for so long trying to get back. It got my heart beating faster and made my arm bleed more than it normally would have. It's not serious."

"Let me look at it, Skylar."

"No, Mom. It's fine. You don't need to worry."

"And you don't need to go back to the marshes." Dad glares at me, daring me to challenge this decision.

"Where are we going to get the berries, then? What about the business?"

"We'll find other ways to make a living, but we don't need you to risk your life for it."

"I'm not at risk. This is the first time in years I've gotten more than a scratch while berry picking, and—"

"And next time it could be worse. You're not going back to the marshes, Skylar. That's final."

"Fine." I stand and head towards the bedroom Mandy and I share, leaving my dinner untouched.

My bed creaks as I sink onto it and lie back. I'm exhausted, but my mind is racing too much for me to sleep. I'm actually kind of glad that my family found out about the arda berries. If I can stay out of sight for a while and the king can't find me, maybe he'll forget about me. Now I have an excuse to stay home that won't raise questions.

I'm just starting to drift off when Mandy comes into the room, bandages and a bowl of water in her hand. "Mom thought you might still want to take care of that cut." I give her a small smile and sit up. "Do you want me to help you?"

I hesitate. I share a lot of things with Mandy that I never tell anyone else. I can trust her with a secret, but will she keep this one? "Promise not to tell Mom and Dad?"

"Tell them what?" She eyes me with furrowed brows. Slowly, I roll up my sleeve, trying to keep the pain from showing in my face. Her eyes widen as the gashes are revealed. "The knightcrawlers actually got you?" she says in a scared whisper.

"It was just one. I can usually get away, but I was cornered this time."

Mandy places the bowl on the stack of books beside my bed and starts gently washing the cuts, staring at me intently, her eyebrows raised in concern. Her eyes are like Dad's, grey speckled with blue. In the moonlight from the window, they look like the starry sky outside. "You need to tell Mom and Dad about this." Now I start to worry. Mandy doesn't keep secrets if she thinks it's something really serious.

"No, it would just make them worry for nothing. I'm not going to the marshes anymore, so it doesn't really matter."

We're silent as Mandy wraps my injured arm in bandages. Finally, she finishes, then stands and says, "If it gets infected and we need to tell our parents, I'm not going to lie for you." A smile spreads across my face. I knew I could count on her.

9

Another Market Day

Skylar

For the next few weeks, I use any possible excuse to stay inside. I never even step out of the house just in case the king's guards are looking around in the village. It's safer not to take any chances.

My family is starting to worry about me, though. I usually go outside at every available chance, even taking my books with me to read in a sunny spot. Now I just help with whatever housework I can find to do and read in my room. Well, I pretend to read. I can't concentrate on anything. Every time I try to occupy myself with a book, I just stare at the same page for hours, memories of that day in the palace chasing through my mind. Mandy has noticed. I try to pass it off as nothing, to make it seem like I'm sulking about not being allowed to pick berries, but they seem more suspicious every day. Tonight, while they think I'm asleep, their whispers reach me from the kitchen.

"It's not like her."

"I don't know what could be wrong."

"Could she be getting sick?"

"She definitely needs to get out of the house."

"Mandy, she talks to you the most . . . "

Whatever they're planning, it can't be good. The next morning, I find out I'm right.

"Skylar, how would you like to go to the market today?" Mom asks with an exaggerated smile while everyone sits around the table for breakfast.

"I thought I wasn't allowed to go there until I learned to be less impulsive."

"I'll be going with to keep an eye on you," Mandy tells me, sounding casual but avoiding my eyes. So, they're trying to see if Mandy can wheedle a confession out of me on a walk? Not happening.

"If Mandy's already going, then why do I need to go?"

"I need some baking ingredients, and it will be too much for Mandy to carry on her own."

"Doesn't Dad usually get everything you need when he goes to work?" I raise one eyebrow, trying to communicate my suspicion. But no one is looking at me.

"The cart broke on my way home last night, so I need to fix it today," Dad says over his bowl of porridge. They certainly planned this well.

"Wouldn't fixing the cart be a two-person job? I could probably be of more help here than in the market."

Mom now furrows her brows in annoyance, finally staring directly into my eyes. "Skylar, we can handle everything here. We need you to help your sister. Besides, you need to get out of the house. You've been cooped up too long." I've run out of reasons not to go, so I grudgingly relent. Maybe the king has lost interest by now.

* * *

Mandy's questions begin as soon as the door closes behind us. "What's been going on with you lately?"

"Subtle, Mandy, really subtle."

"Subtilty is a waste of time. And stop avoiding the question."

"I'm fine."

"No, you're not. You haven't left the house in weeks and you hardly want to do anything. You don't even read anymore. You haven't been your-self ever since you got attacked by that knightcrawler. I was beginning to think you were getting sick because of that wound, and I almost told Mom and Dad about it."

"Don't! It has nothing to do with the cut. I just don't see the point of going out if I can't go berry picking."

She rolls her eyes. "When did you start letting our parents' rules pre-vent you from finding your *excitement*?"

If only you knew, Mandy.

"Mom and Dad never approve of the things I find exciting. I'm tired of arguing with them."

"So, you're saying you've given up? That's not like you, Skylar. Can't you just tell me what's wrong? You usually tell me everything."

"No, I don't."

Mandy becomes quiet. She must think I'm talking about the berry picking. I wish that was the only thing I meant.

We're silent for a long time as we make our way to the marketplace. I keep my eyes focused on the ground as we enter the busy town square, attempting to become invisible in the crowd. I know there wouldn't be any nobility here who would recognise me from the arena, but the servants they send to do their errands might have seen me. Mandy notices my behaviour.

"You get annoyed when the rest of us try to be inconspicuous like that."

"Shut up and let me act weird for once."

"You're always weird. It's when you act normal that I get worried." She smirks, and I give her a playful shove.

We start to do our shopping, and at first it seems like a normal day. Then the commotion starts. A carriage drives into the village, causing everyone to stare. No one rich enough to own a carriage would ever go to a marketplace themselves. Everyone is even more surprised when two palace guards get down from the driver's seat. They immediately head towards the Mistem stands in the middle of the square and start causing chaos. They destroy displays and overturn stands while the Mistems scatter and nearby Haeltons watch with condescending smiles. This happens sometimes, when the king is collecting more funds for the war from the Mistems. Haeltons always enjoy making a show of it. But this time it's a ruse. The guards never take anything, and their eyes are darting around the marketplace. One of them was with the king when he took me to the palace. They're looking for something—or someone. I can guess who, though I hope I'm wrong.

"Skylar?" Mandy whispers at my side. When I turn to her there's terror shining in her wide grey eyes. "Please don't try to be a hero this time." On other occasions I've tried to stop Haelton guards from damaging Mistem property. Not this time.

I shake my head. "Let's get out of sight." Mandy's mouth opens in surprise, but she doesn't argue. We quickly duck into a warehouse filled with goods that a Haelton shop owner is waiting to sell.

Mandy points out a stack of flour sacks in the corner. "Climb!" she mouths, and we immediately head towards it. Mandy reaches it first, and

I'm about to follow her up when something suddenly blocks the light from the door.

"Skylar of Marshwall?" a booming voice asks. Crud. I wish I had my spear. Mandy is barely visible in the dim light, her pale skin and hair blending in with the white sacks, but obviously the guard can see me. I turn, looking as dignified and in-control as possible, my face a mask that covers the fear.

"Yes?" I respond calmly, though my heart is thudding in my chest.

The guard seems more like a messenger than a warrior as she dips her head in a respectful bow. "His Majesty, King Roland of Vexenta, extends his greetings to you, and invites you to return with us to the palace in Respenda."

I respond just as formally. "Give my regards to His Majesty, but I am afraid I will have to decline his invitation." I try to walk past the guard and out of the warehouse, but she grabs my arm. Suddenly she is much less polite.

"Perhaps I should have said 'summons'. Our orders were to return with you, or not to return at all." So, he hasn't forgotten. But I have no intention of going back to the palace.

I try to break free from the guard's grasp using the twisting motion that worked so well in my last market scuffle, but palace warriors are trained well, and she isn't fazed by my escape attempt. Her grip on my arm never loosens. I try fighting in other ways. I kick and struggle with all my might while the guard tries to restrain me. Soon, seeing that I'm not going to come easily, her partner runs over to help. Now it's two against one, but I keep fighting.

Suddenly, Mandy jumps down from her place on top of the flour sacks, tackling one of the guards and screaming, "LEAVE MY SISTER ALONE!" The guard she tackled draws his sword while the other tries to pull me back.

His sword is aimed at Mandy's neck. He's going to kill her! "STOP!" I scream, my voice shrill with panic. Everyone freezes and looks at me. The female guard has both my arms pinned behind my back and I'm panting from exertion, but I lift my head and try to seem as dignified and commanding as possible. "Don't hurt my sister. I'll go with you, and I won't fight. Just leave her alone."

The male guard smirks triumphantly as he sheaths his sword. "Deal." With that, they begin to usher me towards the carriage they left in the middle of the square.

"Skylar, no!" Mandy runs after us, still seeming intent on freeing me.

"Mandy," I try to sound calm. I don't think these Haeltons will honor our deal if Mandy keeps getting in the way. "Don't worry. I'll be fine. Just go home and tell Mom and Dad what happened. Tell them not to worry, I can take care of myself."

Mandy continues to stare and follows us as the guards lead me to the carriage and force me in. As the door shuts, one of them pulls a padlock from his pocket and locks me in. There's no escape. I stare at the floor, dreading what will happen next. I'm not afraid for myself. I knew this could happen, and maybe there's still a way out of this. But I'm scared for my family. None of them should be hurt because I attracted too much attention. As the carriage begins to move, my gaze is pulled to the window, watching as Mandy turns and sprints toward home, quickly vanishing into the crowd. I hope no one follows her. I hope the Haeltons still don't know where we live, and my family will be safe. There will be a lot to explain when I get home. If I get home. Turning away from the window, I shrink back against the seat. No one on the street can see me, and this time I don't see the foreboding road the carriage rumbles over.

10

What Now?

Mandy

M y mind is racing as fast as my feet while I run down the road towards home. I never slow my pace. I can't; the panic and fear won't let me. What did those palace guards want with Skylar? What did that female one say before they took her away? The king wanted to see her? What would the king want with my little sister? How would he even know she existed?

Dad is out front greasing the wheels of our cart as I come within sight of the house. He decided to do that last night so that it would look like he's fixing the cart and Skylar wouldn't have an excuse to avoid going to the market today.

Now I see why she wanted to stay home.

Dad looks up as he hears me coming, and his eyes widen when he sees that I'm alone.

"Where's Skylar? What happened? What's wrong?"

I can barely get the words out as I screech to a halt and gasp for air. "Skylar . . . guards . . . couldn't stop them . . . "

Mom comes bursting out of the house, wiping her dough-covered hands on her apron as she comes toward us. "What's going on?"

Finally, I manage to catch my breath. "Two palace guards captured Skylar in the marketplace! They locked her into a carriage and took her away! One of them said something about the king wanting to see her at the palace!"

"WHAT?!" Dad's eyes are blazing with fear and furry, and Mom's face falls in devastation. Neither of them would blame me for what happened—you can't do anything against Haelton guards—but I can't help feeling guilty. I should never have kept a secret from them.

"I don't know why they might have wanted her, but it must have something to do with the night she got lost. She was hiding something. That cut she got was from a knightcrawler, not a tree branch." I'm nearly crying from the guilt and the worry for what will happen to Skylar.

"Why didn't you tell us this sooner?"

"Skylar said it wasn't anything to worry about. She said she just got cornered and I thought it wasn't a problem then."

"I have to go get her." Mom and I both look at Dad in horrified shock.

"You can't!" Now Mom is nearly in tears. "They're taking her to the palace! You could be killed for going there without permission. And if the king is sending guards after Skylar, do you really think he'll let her go easily?"

"I have to try to get her back. We can't just leave her."

"Skylar said she could take care of herself and we shouldn't worry." Desperation makes my voice sound strained.

"Every time we let her do something on her own, she gets into trouble. I can't just wait around to see if she's alright."

"Please be careful. I can't stand to lose both you and Skylar in one day." The tears start to roll down Mom's cheeks as she clings to him, and I'm barely holding back my own tears.

"I'm always careful. You two just wait here and keep yourselves safe." Dad heads off down the road to Respenda, and Mom and I go into the house, locking the door behind us. Neither of us speak, each lost in our own thoughts. Skylar did something to get herself into trouble, and now Dad's putting himself in danger to help her. If Skylar survives this, I'm going to kill her for scaring all of us.

11

The King's Purpose

Skylar

The carriage draws near to the castle, and I wonder where they will take me. Last time the king wanted to charm me as a guest, but now I'm a prisoner that he wants to kill. My quarters likely won't be so comfortable as before. He'll probably lock me in some dank stone dungeon.

Soon we pull up to the large, imposing front doors. Wait, the front doors? The main entrance that the king and important visitors use? Shouldn't there be a separate entrance for prisoners and other *lowly* people who are taken into the palace? But the guards remove the padlock from my door casually and open it with the same respectful, attentive motions they used when they were ushering in the king, as if this were all normal. They stand on either side of the carriage door, leaving a clear path in front of me, acting like the escort for a royal visitor. What's going on? I step down onto the cobblestone walkway leading to the stairs and debate making a break for it, but the guards quickly step in beside of me, so close that they block my escape.

It's even more confusing when we reach the doors and the footmen who open them bow. They actually bowed to me! Are they mocking me? Their faces look serious . . . The guards don't give me time to ponder this and quickly steer me down the hall. Again, I try to memorize our path. Down the painting-lined hall, turn right, then left, then right again, left, right, two left turns . . . It seems like I've been taken on this route before.

Sure enough, they take me to the same room I was put in during my last visit. After I've gone in, the guards back out of the room with respectfully bent heads, shut the door after them, and leave me alone in the luxurious surroundings. Why am I being brought here? Why are they treating me nicely? Isn't the king still angry, if he was so determined to have me brought back? Is this some sort of cruel joke? Is he trying to make me let down my guard before suddenly throwing me in the arena again? I wouldn't be surprised. A Haelton would probably find something like that funny.

The door opens and every muscle in my body instantly stiffens. I relax slightly when Ann walks in, once again laden with a bundle of fabric. She lays her load on the bed and looks at me, smiling and dipping into a curtsey. "Hello again, My Lady."

I try to sound calm, even cheerful, in my response. "I thought we agreed that you wouldn't call me that."

She smiles sheepishly. "My apologies, Miss."

No one would have told her much, but I have to ask anyway. "Do you know what this is all about? After what happened last time, I didn't think I'd be exactly welcome here."

She shakes her head. "I was only told that you were back, and I was to help you dress again." I look at the dress she brought in. It's different from the last one. It doesn't look like an old dress that was taken out of storage; it looks brand new. The silky fabric has a vibrant sheen to it and the sky-blue colour hasn't had a chance to fade with time. The gold embroidery covering the sleeveless bodice sticks out from the fabric as if it was just stitched on.

I step forward to gather up the clothes. "I'll just change in the bathroom again."

"I'm sorry, Miss, but I'm not allowed to let you do that anymore." I guess they found the hidden undergarments. Reluctantly, I take off my dress and let Ann help me into this new palace costume. I feel more and more restricted as each piece of the outfit goes on. The corset forces me into the straight-backed posture of the nobility, the dress is so tight I feel as though I can't breathe, and the weight of the skirts makes it hard to move my legs. This dress feels like a cage, even with my arms free.

At first, I wonder why the dress is sleeveless, until I look at my bare arms in the mirror. While the cuts from the knightcrawler have almost completely healed, there are still scars on my arm. Haeltons display their battle wounds like jewellery or trophies. I've seen Haeltons walking around in the market, showing off scars or black eyes like it's something to be proud of. If they have very impressive-looking scars, or the story of how they got them is really interesting, they purposefully wear clothes that show them off. Some Haelton women even use makeup to make their scars stand out more. I don't need to do that though; my scars are perfectly visible, deep red against creamy white skin. It's hard to tell if the king wants them to be visible as a warning to others of what he can do if you make him angry, or if he thinks I might want to show off, but either way, I want to get out of this dress as soon as possible.

Once the dress is on, Ann has me sit at the dressing table while she twists my hair into another fancy updo. When she finishes, she turns me toward the mirror, waiting for approval. There are no jewels braided into my hair this time. Instead she put something that looks like a necklace in my hair. It's a thick gold chain going around the top of my head, with a sapphire hanging down from it, resting on my forehead. It almost looks like a crown!

No sooner has Ann finished her work than the instigator of this whole charade enters. Ann steps out as I stand up, expecting the worst.

I can't tell if he's smirking or smiling as he looks me over. "You're even more beautiful than last time, Rose."

"What do you want with me? Why did you have me brought here?"

He chuckles, and I feel blood rushing to my cheeks. "Not one to exchange pleasantries, are you?"

"It's a waste of time. Now why am I here?" My annoyance and anger are clear in my voice, but King Roland's content smile doesn't waver.

"I wanted to see you again. And I'm not the only one to have such a desire. Many members of my court were quite impressed by your performance a few weeks ago. They have been asking about you often."

"So what? If their questions were bothering you, couldn't you just tell them to shut up?"

He half smiles and starts pacing in a circle around the room. I turn as he walks so that I'm always facing him. He doesn't look at me much, mostly staring thoughtfully into the distance, but I never take my eyes off him. "Yes, I could easily silence the inquiries of my nobles, but that does not silence the questions which run through my own mind. How did this remarkable Mistem girl become a better warrior than many Haelton nobles? Why have we never noticed her before? Are there other Mistems like her?"

He looks at me as he says this last question, as if he wants me to answer it. I cross my arms over my chest. "Why would you care if there are others? Are you running out of soldiers to throw at Mishfont?"

"No, but a ruler must know if there is potential unrest in his country."

"Is that why you brought me back here? You're worried that I'd start a rebellion?"

"No. In fact, I think you might be able to help me prevent such an event."

"*Me*? Work in politics?" I scoff at the thought. "Why?"

"Word has spread about how you stood up for those men in the arena. It seems that the working-class people see you as somewhat of an advocate for them. They would be much more content to see that you have a position of importance."

"You want me to help you make everyone happy so that you don't have to worry about possible uprisings?"

"Nations are strongest when they're united."

"What if I refuse? What if I think things should change? Do you think you can scare me into agreeing? I'm not afraid of you or any threats you might make."

He nods, folding his hands behind his back. "I believe that. I was thinking more along the lines of a mutually beneficial agreement. A deal in which we both receive what we want."

"What could you possibly offer that would make me want to stay here?"

King Roland stops his pacing and turns to me, his eyes intensely fixed on my face. "Everything you've ever wanted." He reaches into his pocket, and I stumble back as if struck when I see what he's holding. A ring. A band of braided gold with a cluster of diamonds on top. An engagement ring. This is worse than anything else I imagined when I was being brought here.

I stare at the ring, then at the king's face. He gazes intently back, his mouth set in a serious line. After a moment, it slowly creeps into a warm, encouraging smile.

"You're kidding, right?"

The king's smile falters a bit at my tone, but he answers as if I were some star-struck girl who couldn't believe something so wonderful could happen to her. "I'm quite serious. I know it's unconventional, but I believe this could be a good thing. My court agrees. Those two men you saved from the arena aren't the only ones who have expressed concern with current political standings. It seems that some of the country folk who profit less from the war and see less of it are becoming tired. They simply don't understand the way the military functions. We needed to find way to silence them or placate them. And then I found you, Rose Blossom, and it seems that all our problems could be solved with you as my queen."

"And what if I don't want to be a queen?"

Now his smile is completely gone. His brow furrows in confusion. "Why wouldn't you? Most women would give anything for what I'm offering you. Even noblewomen would be prepared to fight each other over this."

"They're Haeltons, they'd fight over anything. I'm not like any of them. All I want is to leave this palace and never come back. I doubt you would ever give me that."

He puts the ring back in his pocket, his face fallen and eyes downcast. "It seems we have conflicting desires, then. But you would have to be a fool not to see the benefits of my offer. Take some time to think this over. Perhaps you will change your mind."

As he heads out the door, I get the final word. "Don't count on it, *Your Majesty*." He slams the door behind him. I sink onto one of the plush couches feeling like I won some sort of battle, but it doesn't last long. King Roland isn't going to let me go, but I can't stand the thought of staying. He thinks he's offering me every girl's dream, when all he's offering is a fancy cage.

12

A New Idea

Roland

Fuming, I storm down the hall away from Skylar's room, servants and guards jumping out of my way as I go. I head to my throne room and slump into the carved gold chair on the front dais, my thoughts smoldering. She rejected me. I never thought that a noble title could be used disrespectfully, but the way Skylar said 'Your Majesty' as I left made it sound like an insult. I offered her the world, more than any other country girl could ever dream of having, and she recoiled from the ring like it was poison. Is she really that happy with her country life, or does she simply hate me that much?

"Your Majesty?" I hate it when guards interrupt my brooding.

"What is it?" I snap.

"One of the kitchen staff bumped into an intruder skulking around the grounds."

Some people pick the worst times to get on my nerves. "Bring him in."

To my surprise it isn't some daring Haelton miscreant that they drag in front of me; it's a Mistem! He looks middle-aged and is wearing plain clothes that belong in a small country village. His grey eyes are wide and fearful as he's thrown to his knees at the foot of my throne. What could possibly have brought him here? "Explain yourself!" I command, making the Mistem jump. His mouth moves like he's trying to stammer out an explanation, but no sound comes out. I glare in frustration. "Take my advice, Mistem. I'm not the most patient man when it comes to law breakers on the best of days, and this is not a good time. We'll both be much happier if you quit wasting my time. Now!"

Something I said seems to give the Mistem a new sense of purpose, as he straightens up and quickly blurts, "I'm looking for my daughter!" He's shaking in terror.

"What interest would I have in a Mistem's country brat?"

"I don't know, but my older daughter said that your men took her sister from the market this morning!"

Oh, wait. Isn't the girl who just rejected me a country Mistem? I put on a small, pensive smile. "Now that I think of it, I might know where your daughter is. Is she a rather unique girl, with sky-blue eyes and a fiery spirit of determination? A girl by the name of Skylar?"

The Mistem's eyes grow wider with every word I say, though a flicker of anger shows beneath the fear. "Where is she? What have you done to her?" The guards have to hold him back as he lunges toward me. Pretty brave for a Mistem. Maybe it's a family trait.

"Relax. Your daughter is safe and comfortable." This does little to calm the Mistem, but he stops struggling against the guards. "I simply wanted to see her again after the excitement of her last visit."

"Her last visit? What do you mean?" His voice is rising in panic.

"Did she not tell you about the previous time I invited her here? Pity, it's quite a story. Perhaps you will hear it later, though." An idea strikes me. "For now, you might be able to help me."

He becomes so pale that I can almost see straight through him. "H— Help you? What could I possibly help you with, Sire?"

"Solving a slight disagreement between your daughter and myself."

"W—What? If you're angry with her, of course. J—Just let me talk to her, I—I can –"

I cut him off with a dismissive wave of my hand and turn to the guards. "Take him to the arena. See that he has . . . A good view of the action." The guards smile knowingly, and escort out the Mistem, ignoring his attempts at confused protests. I feel a twinge of guilt doing this, but I can't think of a better way. Skylar has no interest in rewards and no fear for threats against herself. I need to try a different tactic, and this seems like the only way to convince her.

13

A Battle of Wills

Skylar

A bowing guard opens the door to find me at one of the large bedroom windows. I quickly step away from the firmly locked latch I was trying to open. "King Roland wishes to speak with you, My Lady."

"We've already spoken. I haven't changed my mind, and unless the king has changed his, there's nothing for us to say to each other."

"Please, just come with me." Sighing, I follow him, preparing myself for another stand-off while searching for an opportunity to escape.

The guard leads me back to the balcony overlooking the arena. The king is standing by the edge, his signet ring looking dull and cold on his hand as it rests on the shaded railing. He turns as the door opens, smiling slightly at the sight of me. I don't trust that smile. I plant my feet just past the threshold of the door and cross my arms over my chest. "What?"

He beckons me over with a wave of his hand. "Come."

I stay put. "Why?"

"There's something you will want to see."

"I doubt it."

"Trust me."

"I don't trust anything you say." I hiss, but I walk to the front corner of the balcony that's farthest from the king. I look out on the arena. All the seats are empty this time, so this isn't another *entertainment*. The sandy pit in the centre looks deserted too; at least, most people would think it is. I've practiced looking for small things hidden in shadows for years while berry picking, and I quickly spot the Mistem hiding in the shadow of a wall. "DAD!" I shout before I can stop myself. At the sound of my voice, Dad looks up and sees me on the balcony. It's hard to see him from this distance, but from the way he stumbles and nearly falls back against the wall, I know he's shocked to see me like this. I don't blame him.

The king grins maliciously, but the smile doesn't reach his eyes. "It seems your father has been trespassing. I'm not angry, though. He's kindly agreed to help me."

"If you think this is going to make me change my mind . . . "

His grin widens. "You haven't seen what else will be in the arena yet." He motions to someone hidden from view, and enormous gates across the arena from my dad begin to open. My eyes pop and my mouth drops at the sight of the creature that emerges. It's something I've only ever seen in my books. A megaline! It's a giant, cat-like creature, bigger than our house. The spear-sized claws and teeth are hidden, for the moment, beneath the golden fur of its paws and mouth. It lunges forward but jerks back with a thundering crash. It's restrained by two gigantic chains leading from a thick iron collar around its neck back through the gates it was hidden behind. I don't think I've ever felt true fear before this moment, but now my heart is pounding, and my brain is numb. All that exists is the scene in front of me, and the monster beside me who caused it.

"You know what you can do to save him." The king's voice is venomously silky.

I whip around to face him, my fist colliding with his face as I turn. "You're a sick, twisted monster!" I yell as I dive at the guard, who's still standing by the door. Before anyone can react, I grab the guard's sword, sprint back across the balcony, and vault over the railing. This time, I don't black out. I'm ready for the landing and roll with the impact, then I quickly stand and run towards Dad.

Seeing movement, the giant cat tries to swipe at me, but I'm out of its reach. It strains to move forward, and there are faint cracks and shouts from inside the megaline's cage. How long will the restraints hold?

I reach Dad and his eyes dart over me, taking in my dress, my hair, the scars on my arm, and the sword I'm holding. "Skylar... What–? How–?"

"I'll explain later, but we have to get out of here now!"

"How? There are guards at every door, not to mention that thing!" He points frantically to the deadly mountain of golden fur, just visible through the cloud of dust it kicks up while fighting against the chains. I look between it and the seats above us, and suddenly I have an idea.

"Try to distract the megaline. Move around, let it see you, but stay just out of its reach."

"Are you kidding? I'm staying as far away from that thing as possible!"

"Trust me, Dad! I have a plan, but we need to get it straining against its chains."

"What are you going to do?" His brow furrows and the panic in his voice rises.

"You'll be happier not knowing that for now. Just distract the megaline!" With that, I take off, running along the wall of the arena toward the gates.

"Skylar!" Dad shouts after me, but I'm already far enough away that I can pretend not to hear. Left with no other choice, he begins to run around the far side of the arena, attracting the megaline's attention, but always staying just out of reach of the swiping claws.

When I reach the open gates, the guards on the other side are working frantically to keep the rings attached to the megaline's chains from being ripped out of the wall. They hammer large hooks through the giant links and into the wall, but each one almost immediately bursts back out. When I run in, they're too distracted and confused to stop me as I head for one of the rings. Shoving the point of the sword into a crack in the wall, I use it as a lever to loosen the chain. With the megaline straining against its bonds, the ring easily pops free from the wall with a loud crack and a spray of rubble. Realizing what I'm doing, the guards flee from the cage. The other ring is coming loose even faster now. I step through the gates and motion to Dad to run. He dives into the shadows as I free the other ring from the wall.

The megaline is loose.

It runs toward Dad, roaring in triumph as it discovers its freedom. I drop the sword, run out of the cage and start yelling and waving, attracting the beast's attention. It turns toward me, and I dodge as it swipes. Seeing what I'm doing, Dad again starts distracting the megaline. From either side of the arena, we take turns calling the attention of the feline, diving to the ground when the wildly swinging chains come near us. Now it's time to get out of here.

"Dad!" I yell when it's my turn to be the distraction. I point to the chain closest to him and motion for him to climb it. He looks at me as if I've lost my mind, but we have no other options. He grabs the chain as it swings towards him, and I do the same with the one closest to me. Fighting against the momentum of the chains as the confused creature starts turning in tight, rapid circles trying to reach us, we slowly make our way up. Once we get onto its back, we hold on to the collar so hard our knuckles go completely white.

"Now what?" Dad yells over the growling hisses and thundering footfalls of the megaline as it turns its attention to the walls and seats barring the way to true freedom.

"Let's see if we can steer this thing!" I grab a chain from one side of the collar and start leaning in the opposite direction. Dad takes hold of it too, leans with me, and we slowly force the megaline's head to face the seats opposite the king's balcony. We drop the chain and grab the collar again as, without much encouragement, the beast lunges forward and starts climbing. We duck down as close to its body as we can as rubble starts to fly in the wake of the megaline's claws. Soon it's at the top of the wall, and we fight to stay on as it jumps to the ground below.

It pauses for a moment, looking around. Megalines are used to wide open spaces, but we're in the palace grounds with a sprawling city just beyond the walls. It spots the one area that looks uninhabited, the forest I escaped into last time, and charges straight for it. It could carry us miles away if we don't get off. But as I grip the iron collar and listen to the chains clinking on either side of us, I realize we can't just leave the megaline like this. It's cruel to tie up wild animals. Spotting the padlock used to hold on the collar, I grab one of the chains as it swings towards me. There's a sharp spike on the end that held the ring in the wall. I jam the spike hard into the keyhole, and the lock falls apart. Then the collar falls off its captive.

"Jump!" I shout to Dad, and we both launch off the megaline's back just before it crashes into the forest, guided by a natural homing instinct to whatever place it calls home. Dad and I quickly get up from where we landed and stare at each other, relief flooding our faces. Then, reminded of where we are by shouts coming from the arena, we run into the forest and start heading home before the king can send his guards after us.

14

Truth be Told

Skylar

When we're far enough away from the palace, Dad and I slow our pace to a walk. I'm exhausted and sore; the way Dad is slouching tells me he feels the same. We don't speak, but I'm sure we're both asking ourselves the same question: now what do we do?

I look down at the dress I'm wearing. The skirt is peppered with small tears, the hem is tattered, and some of the seams on the bodice have started to split. I look over at Dad and see that his face and hands are covered in scratches. I know I don't look much better; my skin stings wherever bits of flying rubble hit me, and I know my hair is a mess. I'm surprised the necklace-crown stayed on my head. Ann must have attached it very well. Dad keeps glancing over at me, mostly looking at my scars. There's no fake story I could tell that would explain all of this.

We're halfway home when I can't stand the silence anymore. A thought strikes me that makes my heart start racing again. "Dad, what were you doing at the palace? Did the king find out where we live?"

To my relief, he shakes his head. "I went there to try and get you out. I was looking around the back when someone came out of a door right by me and called for guards when they saw me." If I weren't so tired, I would be astonished. I thought I was the only one who could be driven to take risks.

We walk in silence the rest of the way home, keeping away from the main road where I would attract too much attention in my dress. The sun sets as we walk, and it's dark by the time we get home.

Mom and Mandy immediately run out to greet us. Mom can't seem to decide who to hug first, so she puts an arm around both of us. "I'm so glad you're safe! We didn't know if we'd ever see you again! I—" Her next words are drowned out by her tears of relief. Mandy doesn't say anything as she joins the family group hug. When she meets my eye, her mouth twitches and she looks torn between anger and relief. But then she notices what I'm wearing and steps back.

"Skylar, what–?" Mom then steps back too, and they both stare, dumbfounded.

"Get in the house," Dad says, as he ushers us all toward the door. He takes my arm and guides me inside, as if he's afraid that I'll run off. When we enter the kitchen, he forces me to sit down at the table. Mom and Mandy sit down too, as Dad takes a seat across from me and looks me straight in the eyes. "I think it's time you stopped hiding things from us."

I take a deep breath and start telling the whole story. Everything, right from the day the king first saw me in the marshes. When I start telling about the arena fight with the megaline, Dad puts in a few words now and then. As I talk, Mom's hands cover her mouth and her eyes widen so much they look like they might pop out of her head. Mandy simply looks stunned. But Dad keeps his eyes on the table, becoming more solemn and grave as the story goes on. When I finish, there's a long pause before anyone speaks.

"The king actually proposed to you?" Mandy's voice is hardly more than a whisper. I nod. "Why didn't you accept?"

"Why would I? I don't like the way he's running the country, but he wanted to marry me so that everyone would be content with keeping it the same. It's a terrible idea."

"At least he would be happy."

"And what about everyone else? Besides, I don't want to marry someone and then constantly be afraid for my own safety and yours."

"How safe are we now, though?" Mom finally takes her hands away from her mouth. "If the king is that angry, and we live so close to the capital . . ."

"We have to leave." Dad doesn't take his eyes off the table as he speaks. We all gape at him.

"Dad . . . " I want to protest, but he raises a hand to silence me.

"We aren't safe here anymore. I know you don't like running away from conflict," he looks pointedly at me, "but this is a fight you can't win."

My gaze slips down into my lap and I realise that I've been crumpling the skirt of the dress in my hands. I don't want our family to be uprooted, but Dad is right. If we stay here, the king will come back, and who's life will he threaten then? Besides, this doesn't mean I'm accepting defeat. If I can't win this fight, neither will the king. Neither of us will get what we want, and neither of us will win. Sometimes it's best to end fights that way. Slowly, I nod, and we begin to prepare for the long journey ahead.

15

A New Plan

Roland

L ast night's events still baffle me as the carriage clatters down the country road. I realize Skylar is a good fighter, but to defeat a megaline! Though, she didn't really defeat it; she controlled it. She found a way to use my own weapon against me, which is more impressive. I'm used to doing things my own way and being in control of almost everything, as it should be for a king, but I don't think it will work that way with Skylar. It's time to try something different.

I finger the package lying on the seat beside me. Skylar might be more open to making an agreement if I come with a peace offering. The contents of the package are already hers, I'm only bringing the clothes she left behind yesterday, but I'll let her keep the dress she ran away in as a gift.

We're drawing near to the house where my spy says she lives. Before I met Skylar, I never noticed the talents that Mistems have, but now I can appreciate how well they can move around without being noticed. Sending a Mistem servant to follow Skylar and her father worked incredibly.

I order the carriage to stop when the house comes into view. Skylar likely won't be on her guard so much if I come alone. I step out into the early morning mist, tuck the package under my arm, and walk the rest of the way to the small country house.

There is a lot of activity in front of her home, considering how early it is. There's a cart parked by the door with a pile of various items loaded onto it. A Mistem I recognise as Skylar's father is standing on the cart, stacking more items onto it. I don't recognise the two women handing objects to him from the ground, but I know the older one must be Skylar's mother.

The other is likely her sister; the guards who brought Skylar to the palace said she had a sister with her.

A moment later Skylar herself emerges from the house. She's wearing the same outfit she had on when I first saw her in the marshes, the long sleeves rolled down almost to her wrists despite the warmth of the morning. Why do Mistems try to hide their scars? They act as if they are some type of contagious rash. I'll admit that the scratches covering her face do resemble a rash from a distance, but knowing how she got them, they make her look courageously beautiful, like an accomplished warrior. This effect is further established by the spear she's carrying, even though it's the simple sharpened stick she was using to pick berries in the marshes. I can't see her father's face as she puts the spear onto the cart, but I can guess that he doesn't approve, because she immediately defends her actions.

I can just hear her from where I'm standing. "If there's trouble, we'll need something to defend ourselves!" Her father doesn't argue; he seems to be in a hurry.

No one has seen me yet, so I have a chance to look again at the cart and all the items they're packing onto it. Everything in their house seems to be on there. Are they trying to run? That won't do.

I walk quickly forward, into full view of the Mistem family. "Going somewhere?"

16

Negotiations

Skylar

M om, Dad, and Mandy all freeze, but I whip around to face the king. What is he doing here? How did he find us? "What do you want?" I want to scream, to yell, to make King Roland regret stopping his carriage by the marshes when he first saw me. I rest my hand on the spear in the cart, a clear warning.

He doesn't come any closer. The king isn't smirking this time; he doesn't seem over-confident and controlling like before. He's also alone. Is he coming peacefully, or does he think he can handle me without guards? Knowing Haeltons, I doubt it's the former, but I can't be sure.

King Roland holds up a hand. "I'm here to return something of yours." His eyes are fixed on me as his other hand holds out a package wrapped in brown paper. I want to take my spear with me, but Dad seems to know what I'm thinking and grabs the other end of it. He meets my eyes steadily, his brow creasing in a stern expression. Reluctantly, I let go of my spear before striding towards King Roland and wordlessly snatching the package from his hands. He watches as I partially unwrap it. It's the clothes I was wearing in the market yesterday. Why would he bother returning these?

I'm not sure what to do, so I say the first thing that comes to my mind. "I suppose you want the dress back, then?"

He half smiles, but not in the condescending way he did yesterday. "No, keep it. Consider it a gift."

So, he's giving me a torn-up wearable cage as a gift. Does he think that will make me happy? "Thank you," I say without sincerity.

I'm about to walk away, but he puts a hand out to stop me. "I also want to speak with you." He glances over at my family before adding, "Privately."

I'm not sure what to do; this could be a trap. I look over at my family, standing like statues as they watch us with wide, fearful eyes. At least the king won't be near them if I accept his invitation to talk. "Fine, just give me a minute." He nods, and I walk over to my family.

Dad jumps off the cart as I approach. I know they could hear what the king and I were saying, and they all start to protest at once, but I cut them off. I keep my voice low and tell them, "Go in the house and keep the door locked until I get back. Don't worry," I add as mouths open to protest. "He doesn't have any guards or weapons or creatures he could threaten us with here. I'll be fine."

Mom hugs me. "Just promise you'll be careful," she breathes.

"I promise," I whisper back. With that, she lets go and Dad and Mandy each get a turn to hug me as well. They enter the house, constantly looking over their shoulders until the door closes behind them.

I turn back to King Roland, and suddenly have an idea. "I know where we can go to talk." He doesn't say anything but silently falls into step beside me as I lead him to the trail I always take to the marshes. Once we're out of the open fields and in the cover of the trees, I'll have plenty of chances to lose him there, if I need to.

As we walk, I look over at him, noticing the change in his appearance for the first time. He's not wearing a military uniform anymore. His clothes, a suit made of expensive copper-coloured material and cut to fit him perfectly, could almost be considered casual for a nobleman. There's a bruise on his cheek where I hit him, and the dark circles under his eyes give the impression that he slept as badly as I did last night. Feeling my stare, he glances over, and I quickly look away. As I do so, his signet ring catches my eye, glinting faintly in the early-morning sun. He's moved it onto the middle finger of his right hand, and I can see why. There's a deep red line around his ring finger; like he was gripping something so tightly that his ring cut into it.

"I know that I didn't make a very good impression when you were at the palace . . . " he begins.

I laugh humourlessly. "That's an understatement."

He takes a breath before continuing. "I hope that maybe we can start over."

"What do you mean, 'start over'? We can't change the past; we can't erase what happened. And I can't forget it, either."

"I know, I'm not asking you to. But if you could give me a chance—"

"A chance for what?" I face him, my cheeks flushing and my voice rising. "A chance to get on my good side? You had that chance. You could have left me alone and forgotten about me, but you didn't."

He shakes his head. "I couldn't simply forget about you. Not after everything I witnessed. I'm asking you to give me a chance to win your heart, to show you that this is a good idea, to—"

I stop dead in my tracks and slap him. He doesn't react but grabs my wrist before I can hit him again and holds it tightly as he gazes steadily into my eyes. He doesn't look angry, but I certainly am. "How dare you suggest that, after what you did!" I yell in his face. He doesn't flinch; he doesn't show any emotion as his calm golden eyes meet mine. After a minute he lets go of my wrist and I quickly turn away, blinking back hot tears of rage.

"I know that what I did was terrible. I'm a warrior. I learned from childhood to handle issues violently. I realize that, with you, such tactics were a mistake. I hope that someday you might be able to forgive me."

"No." I'm not yelling anymore, but my anger is still obvious in my voice. I look back, meeting his gaze. "You tried to kill me, then you threatened to kill my father. That's not forgivable."

He glances at the ground for a moment. "I would never have actually released the megaline. I was sure you would have seen that you had no fighting chance against the thing and would have given in." He looks back at me. "I underestimated you."

"Obviously." I fold my arms over my chest. "You've already threatened my safety and the safety of my family twice in less than a month. I can't trust you, and I could never even consider loving someone I can't trust."

"Then give me a chance to earn your trust, to show you that I can change."

I turn on my heel and keep heading down the rough dirt path. The king matches my rapid pace. I don't look at him as I speak. "I doubt you could, Sire."

"I can prove you wrong." He puts a hand on my shoulder and spins me around to face him. "You told me that you wanted things to change in Vexenta. Given the unrest which has been building among the people, I'm beginning to think we need that change. I can make it happen. You have the ideas and I have the power to bring them into reality. Let me show you that things, and people, can change." His voice almost sounds pleading. His shoulders have slumped; all the well-bred posturing is gone. For a moment he isn't the angry warrior-monarch that caused so much trouble for us, just a normal person, begging for a second chance.

I look down, considering what he said. Is he serious about using my ideas? This might be the only chance I get to really make a difference, to make sure that everyone is treated fairly. I've tried to make small changes just in our village before, but Mistems are too shy to demand to be noticed, and Haeltons won't pay attention to us unless we force them to. Now I have a chance to make a difference throughout the country . . .

I meet his gaze again, and my voice is calm and determined as I answer him. "Alright, Your Majesty. Show me that you're true to your word and change the way you run this country."

He straightens up smiles. It's not a condescending or triumphant smile, he simply looks happy. "Excellent!" the king exclaims.

"But on one condition."

His smile falters slightly and a look of confusion glances over his face. "Condition?"

"Yes." I throw my shoulders back and try to talk with as much diplomacy as I can muster. "You want a second chance, I will give it to you. You want to work with me to make some changes, I will work with you. But I am not going to suffer through shameless flirtations. If I work with you, it will be strictly professional. Agreed?"

The king is silent for the longest moment, thinking this over. Finally, he makes up his mind. "Agreed."

Our conversation apparently over, we turn around and head back towards the house. We're silent at first, but soon the king speaks again, folding his hands behind his back and returning to his formal, diplomatic mannerisms. "Would you accept an invitation to dinner, then?"

I stop again. "What?!"

He turns to me, and his serious tone makes it sound like he's negotiating a peace treaty with a foreign ruler. "If we're going to work together, you will need to come to Respenda once in a while."

I hesitate. I don't want to go back to the palace, but he's right. That's where all the major political decisions are made, and I can't make much difference if I'm not there. "Fine, but not tonight. I need to talk to my family first."

"Tomorrow, then? I can send a carriage for you in the evening."

"Fine."

He smiles again, and we walk the rest of the way to the house in silence. When we reach the door, he attempts to kiss my hand in a polite, regal farewell, but I pull it away and dart inside. My family looks on in silence as I watch him walk away through the window. Once he's out of sight, I turn to them and begin answering the endless questioning that follows.

17

The Changes Begin

Skylar

W e spend the day unpacking the cart. Now that the king isn't going to threaten us, it's safe to stay here. We couldn't leave anyway, since I'll be going to the palace regularly. Mandy is kind of excited about that. She loves fancy things, although we can't afford them. Ever since childhood she would always look longingly at the windows of Haelton shops where elaborate dresses and accessories were displayed. Of course, the only way she could indulge those desires was by buying extra thread if we had the money and embroidering small designs on a pocket of her clothes or something. Now she eagerly helps me repair the torn gown, so I can wear it to the palace. I hate the idea of wearing it again. I'm tempted to just wear my normal clothes, but Mom insists that I look nice and that I don't openly try to provoke the king.

Mandy runs her hand over the silky skirt, looking for tears we might have missed and letting her hands linger on the soft surface. "I can't believe King Roland actually let you keep this. It's so beautiful, and it looks like it was made specifically for you by an expert seamstress. You'll look like a princess!"

I snort derisively. "I don't want to be a princess, or even a noble woman. I'm only doing this so no Mistem feels the need to cower every time a Haelton goes by."

I study the dress for a moment, thinking, then I take a pair of scissors and start cutting along the seam between the bodice and the skirt.

"What are you doing?" Mandy asks, aghast.

"Making a pocket."

"Why?"

"In case I ever need to bring something with me to the palace."

"Don't most Haelton ladies carry a purse to use for something like that?"

"Yeah, but I'm not them. I like using pockets and I don't want to have to go and buy a purse. Besides, I'll hide it so that no one will notice." Mandy relents and starts working on the hem.

* * *

The next afternoon, I'm kept busy with Mom and Mandy fussing over me, trying to make me look palace-worthy. I sit at the kitchen table while they try to put my hair in a fancy style like the one Ann did. I finger the pocket in the gown and find a bit of pleasure in my little mark of rebellion.

I don't really notice what they're doing, and I don't really care. I don't care what I look like. My mind keeps wandering, wondering what will happen tonight and creating a number of possible scenarios. What if any nobles are there? Will they expect me to make some sort of speech about the changes I want done? How will they react? And if it's just me and King Roland? Will he keep his promise to refrain from flirting with me? Will this turn into another fight? I can't imagine this evening ending well.

I'm pulled from my musings when a hairpin clatters loudly to the floor and Mom starts muttering under her breath in frustration. "Mom, just put it in a simple bun. It'll be a lot easier."

"Yes, but is that really appropriate if you're going to the palace?"

"It'll be fine. I don't really care what my hair looks like, and neither will anyone else."

"Are you sure about that?"

"Yes." At least, I won't care what anyone else thinks.

"I'm sure it will look fine once we put this on her." Mandy says as she emerges from our bedroom—I hadn't even noticed that she went in there. She's holding up the necklace-crown, a gleeful smile plastered on her face. I shake my head vigorously, causing my hair to tumble onto my shoulders as the hairdo Mom was attempting escapes the pins.

"I don't want to wear that."

Mandy looks disappointed. "Why not?"

"I wore it last time because the king wanted me to look 'queenly' when he proposed. I don't want him to get any ideas tonight."

As Mom starts twisting my hair into a simpler style, Mandy sighs and sits beside me at the table, fingering the headpiece. I glance at her dejected face and feel a stab of sympathy. "If you want to wear it, though, that's fine."

Her smile is small, but her eyes are bright with excitement. "Seriously?"

I shrug and return her smile. "Why not?"

"There's no reason for me to wear something like this."

"So? Just have a bit of fun."

Grinning, Mandy puts on the headpiece and, standing in an imitation of the rich Haelton women, she starts talking in her most pompous, mock-noble voice. I laugh, and, to my surprise, I enjoy the little remaining time before we hear a carriage pulling up in front of our house.

I sigh as I stand and head towards the door. "Have fun!" Mom says weakly to my retreating back.

"Maybe," I respond, glad she can't see my rolling eyes. Just before I open the door I turn back to them. "I'll try to be home as soon as possible." Then, with an exchange of final goodbyes, I leave the comfort of my home to face the evening ahead.

When I step outside, I see the carriage waiting for me and a guard holding the door open. For some reason, King Roland is also standing there. He smiles as I approach. "Good evening, Rose!"

"I'm sorry, what did you say, Your Majesty?" I ask sarcastically.

Brows furrowed in confusion, he starts to repeat himself. "I said, 'Good evening, R—" he stops at the glare I give him, then smiles again. " . . . Skylar."

Satisfied, I climb into the carriage, again ignoring his chivalrously extended hand. I don't say anything until the door closes behind him and we start moving. "You know you didn't have to come here. You could have just sent the carriage."

"Yes, that is true, but I wanted to speak with you before your arrival. The nobles are eager to meet you, so some will be at dinner tonight, and there is something I thought you should have before you met them."

My eyes narrow in suspicion as I watch him pull something from his pocket. "What is that?" I ask, starring at the small, glittery object in his hand and backing away as far as my seat will allow.

The king gives me a calm, disarming smile, though it fails to help me relax. "Don't worry, it's not an engagement ring."

Tentatively, I put out my hand and let him place the object into it. He's right, it's not an engagement ring, although it is a ring. I look closely at the design on the flat, round top, the place where the seal of a noble is etched. It's a signet ring. "Why are you giving me this?"

"When we first met you adamantly pointed out that you were not a noblewoman. Since you will be working closely with the nobility and already are practically a member of the court, I thought we should change that, *My Lady*."

He seems a little too satisfied as he says those last two words. I raise my eyes just enough to study the broad curve of his mouth, then turn my gaze away.

I look more closely at the seal on the ring. As with the seals of Haelton nobles, the pictures and symbols on the ring show things of personal significance. The background is dominated by an arda berry tree with a spear drawn diagonally in front of it. In the other direction, making an X with the spear, are three parallel stripes; the scars on my arm seem to prickle as I stare at them. I glance over at the king. He watches me with a confident grin, as if expecting that I'll burst out in gratitude at any moment. How foolish.

"Thank you for the offer, but I don't need this," *or want it*. I try to give back the ring.

The king starts back in surprise, but he quickly regains his composure. "Perhaps you don't yet realize the benefits of having noble status." He smiles as if he's explaining something simple to an ignorant child.

Hiding a scowl, I respond, "I don't think I need a piece of metal to make people listen to me."

He chuckles quietly. "No, you certainly do not, but that is not what I meant. All nobles who help make decisions in court are given a salary."

"So what? I don't need any money." I lie.

He tries again to win me over. "Nobility are also allowed to travel anywhere they want without requiring passports."

For a moment, I'm tempted. I've read about a lot of different places in my books and studied maps showing some of them, imagining what it would be like to go somewhere else. I would love to see more of the world than Marshwall or Respenda. Yet even the promise of being able to see places in more than just my imagination can't convince me to join the ranks of the high-and-mighty Haeltons. Again, I hold out the ring, trying to give it back. "I don't see why I would ever need to travel."

He pushes my hand back. "You can never tell what the future might hold." He studies me for a moment. "I thought someone like you would want to explore the world for the fun of it."

"You thought wrong," I lie through clenched teeth. Slumping back in the seat I turn the ring over in my hand. As it catches the evening light from the window, I notice something odd about it. It looks like it's made of gold, but there's a strange, pinkish tinge to the metal. "What's wrong with the colour?" I wonder aloud.

"Nothing. It's rose gold, for the Blossoming Rose." He looks over at me as if expecting a response, but I clench my jaw and remain silent. He continues. "Unlike some other pieces of jewelry, there are no other metals mixed into this ring to make it cheaper. It's purely beautiful through and through, just like the girl it was made for."

Nice. Poetic. Other girls might be flattered at a speech like that. But I see this ring for what it really symbolizes. A brand, a tag that marks me as the king's, as a member of *his* court, as *his* Lady, *his* guest, the woman he wanted as *his* wife. I refuse to be claimed like this. "I really don't need this," I say as I thrust the ring back at the king. Again, he pushes my hand back.

"Keep it anyway. It's rude to refuse a gift." He smiles as if he's won some sort of battle, but I refuse to be conquered.

With an overly sweet smile and a sarcastic tone, I respond, "In that case, thank you so much. I'll always treasure this." I add maliciously as I shove the ring unceremoniously into the newly-added pocket of my gown. I knew I'd find a use for it. The rest of the trip to the palace is spent in silence, watching the landscape roll past.

18

Noble Minds

Roland

The doors to the dining room open and the hall rings with the sound of chairs scraping on the floor as ten lords and ladies stand to greet us. I motion for Skylar to walk in beside me, but she deliberately stays a few steps behind. Hiding my annoyance, I lead her to the table, flanked on either side by a line of nobles. There are only two seats left unoccupied: a high-backed, throne-like one at the head for me, and the chair just beside me on my right, reserved especially for Skylar. We stand by our seats as I make introductions. All eyes are fixed on Skylar, whose face is frozen in a forced, small attempt at an emotionless aristocratic smile. When I introduce her as 'Lady Skylar' she demurely places her right hand on the table, showing off the ringless fingers. She seems determined to stand apart from the group, despite what's concealed in the hidden pocket of her gown.

We sit down, and immediately servants begin to serve the dinner and drinks. Skylar smiles warmly as she thanks the Mistem servers, but stiffly locks her eyes on her food as soon as the conversation begins. For once, I'm not the main target of all the questions.

Lady Lauretta, a young politician who is close to my own age and sitting next to Skylar, begins by saying what I'm sure everyone is thinking. "We were all quite impressed with your performance in the arena. How did you learn to fight so well?"

"By gathering berries," Skylar answers evasively.

Furrows of confusion appear on the surrounding faces, so I add, "In the marshes," causing impressed murmurs to ripple around the table and earning a blazing glare from Skylar for my helpfulness.

On the other side of Lady Lauretta, her father, Lord Declan, the counsellor in charge of arming the soldiers of Vexenta, calls Skylar's attention away from me. "What sort of weapon do you use on such excursions?"

"Nothing special. Just a spear-sized branch that I carved into a point," she says with a shrug.

Lady Lauretta's face lights up in amazement. "That explains why you chose to use the staff. But why wouldn't you buy a real spear if you were going into a place like that?"

"A Mistem buying weapons? It would raise too many unwanted questions."

A derisive laugh drifts over from the far left end of the table. "Why should you care what a bunch of Mistem cowards think?" Lady Millicent queries.

"Why should I raise needless suspicions in a village where I'm already an outlier?"

"Village? Oh, a country girl. How quaint!" Lady Millicent's mouth is open, as if she wants to say more, but when her eye catches the hard, disapproving frown I give her she immediately falls silent. I've never had much patience where she's concerned. I wish she wouldn't come to palace events like this, but since her father, Lord Xavier, is a prominent member of my council, she often comes with him. She seems to think that she ought to be queen and is constantly trying to catch my attention. It's a fruitless effort, since the only time she does anything remotely interesting is when she tries to get any possible competition *out of the picture*. Of course, her father only encourages her in this. I'm sure that he thinks he should be running the country. It doesn't help that he was head of the council before I came of age, so he practically was ruling it for eight years.

There's a tense pause as everyone looks between the two women. The only sound in the room is made by Lady Millicent's cutlery as she peacefully returns to eating. Skylar has also turned back to her food, her face devoid of expression, so the conversation soon resumes on a safer topic.

"The repairs and changes to the arena are coming along nicely, Your Majesty," Lord Mason, the chief architect, reports.

Skylar perks up. "What changes are being made?"

I answer her with a satisfied smile. "I think it's time we move away from entertainments involving creatures. The arena will now be used in a more constructive manner, for competitions and as a training ground for nobility." I briefly catch Skylar rolling her eyes as she turns back to her food.

"Perhaps you could join our practice sessions, Lady Skylar. I have an excellent idea for a style of training armour which would look amazing with your hair!" offers Lord Mason's fashion-obsessed wife, Lady Scarlett. Skylar says nothing, but gives Lady Scarlett a strained, grimacing smile.

"Yes, you certainly should join us! I would love to see what you can do with a sword." General Chase pipes up. "If more Mistems were like you, I might consider putting them in the army!" Given the encouraging smile on his face, I know he means this to be a compliment, but Skylar seems to take it differently. Her fists clench, causing her knife to scrape across her plate with an ear-splitting screech that causes several people sitting near her to wince.

Taking a breath and regaining her composure, she simply says, "I think that might not be the best idea, General."

"I agree, Lady Skylar," Lord Grant, minister of finance, declares. "It would mean training and feeding a whole other division of soldiers while at the same time preventing a host of Mistems from producing the funds we need. It simply wouldn't be economical."

"Mishfont uses Mistems, and they don't seem to be struggling." Lord Xavier points out.

Seeing the flush in Skylar's face, I quickly intervene. "Mishfont uses them as nothing more than distractions for our soldiers. I think there are better things for Mistems to do in this country."

"Of course, Your Majesty." General Chase falls silent and Skylar's face softens a little as she nods her thanks to me. Then she gets in the last word.

"Anyway, I believe there are more important issues to be discussed."

"What would you suggest, Lady Skylar?" Lady Lauretta asks.

"Yes, what could be more important than expanding our country?" her father adds.

Skylar pauses a moment before responding, her controlled voice thick with determination. "I know that some might think that the most important area in politics is warfare, and that it's better for leaders to be feared than anything else, but I disagree. From what I've seen just in my village, and heard from surrounding areas, the king is too concerned with foreign matters while issues within the country are building up and not being dealt with effectively. I also see prolonged fear leading, not to loyalty, but to hatred and resentment. It only increases the problems within the kingdom."

Before anyone can disagree, Lady Clara, an intelligence officer and scholar, calls Skylar's attention. "That comment you made, Lady Skylar, about warfare being the most important political concern, sounds familiar. Do you read philosophy books?"

"I've had the opportunity to look through a few," Skylar responds non-committally. Lady Clara grins, pleasantly impressed. At her side, her young student, Lord Maverick, has a similar reaction. He doesn't say anything, he never does unless he knows that his words would be intellectual gold, but his eyes shine with admiration. If it weren't for Skylar's apparent apprehension towards Haeltons, I would be worried that he might become competition. However, not everyone seems impressed by Skylar's display of knowledge.

"What does it matter what she's read?" General Chase demands. "Who is she to come in here and start telling us what we should focus on and who we should or shouldn't use as soldiers?" With hands balled into clubs on the table, the general half rises from his seat. Before he can continue his rant, I slam my own fist into the table.

"Sit down, General." I command. Reluctantly, he obeys and falls silent. "I brought Lady Skylar here for a reason, and her suggestions are no more to be disregarded than yours. Before we dismiss her viewpoint, perhaps the Lady would like to explain her position."

All eyes immediately turn to Skylar, and she meets their stares steadily. "As I stated, from the viewpoint of the common people, it appears that when the king gives excessive focus to warfare, issues within his own country are ignored until they become problematic. The actions of the Haelton men who were recently in the arena shows that there is dissatisfaction among the people, that some are tired of this war. Most Mistems are of this opinion, although we usually refrain from voicing such opinions and stirring up unrest. However, that might change with provocation, for example, if Mistems were put in the army." Here her eyes flash toward General Chase. "If you force people to do something that is directly against what they've been taught since childhood, something that's part of their nature, they are more likely to turn on you. Perhaps Mishfont seems to be alright because their Mistems are biding their time and waiting for the opportunity or courage to rebel, or they are working to find a quiet way to change the situation. In either case, I doubt such arrangements would last very long."

Silence follows Skylar's speech as everyone shoots glances around the table, trying to judge the reactions of others. A few seem impressed, others, annoyed, and some look as if they didn't hear a word she said. General Chase seems to take her words as a personal insult, while Lord Grant has a smug half-smile plastered on his face, as if he's won an argument. When they catch one another's eye, this expression causes General Chase to flush with rage. "Do you think we're going to be scared of Mistem uprisings?!" he shouts, standing. "We can crush any resistance they give us!"

"And how much energy and resources will be taken up doing that while Mishfont makes headway into our territory?" Lord Grant demands. "Face it, General, it's a ridiculous notion."

"What would you know, you whimpering excuse for a soldier!"

Now Lord Grant is on his feet as well. "I know you have no idea what your doing, you metal-headed idiot!"

"THAT'S IT!" the general hollers. With a savage growl he launches over the table, sending food flying in all directions, and tackles Lord Grant to the ground with a flying leap. Well, we almost made it to dessert this time.

While the servants begin cleaning up the mess that's a safe distance from the fight, the lords and ladies leave their seats to watch it. Lord Xavier and Lord Declan begin cheering them on while the others take bets and Lady Clara and Lord Maverick calculate odds. I sit back and let them have their fun. I don't notice that Skylar hasn't moved until Lady Lauretta speaks.

"I bet ten gold that the general wins this one. What do you bet, Lady Skylar?"

"Nothing," she responds in an icy tone.

"Not a gambler?"

"No, and honestly, I don't see the point of such behaviour."

"They're just relieving some energy," Lady Lauretta says off-handedly.

"Hmm," is the only response she gets. Skylar's eyes remind me of blue-hot fire. I should probably get her away from this scene.

"Lady Skylar, would you accompany me for a moment?" I ask, standing and extending my hand to her. She nods and stands, ignoring my hand. Lady Millicent is glaring at us, and Skylar notices too, but we both simply meet her eyes with steady gazes and keep walking.

* * *

Skylar waits until the banquet hall door closes before turning to me with a disgusted grimace. "Are they always like that?"

"That was fairly typical, yes. It's an accepted method for settling some disputes. I hope you aren't too shaken up by their outburst."

"I'm not shaken up, I'm just wondering how anything gets done here if every government gathering disintegrates into something like that." She gestures to the door. As if to emphasize her point, a crash emanates from the banquet hall, followed by cheers.

"When court is in session, they hold back the insults."

"That's insane. I can see a few heated arguments ending in violence, but all of them?!"

"We are warriors. What were you expecting?"

"That maybe the people running our country could find diplomatic solutions to their problems?"

I can't help but smirk at her naivety. "A display of strength is considered diplomatic." Skylar mumbles something under her breath, and I catch the word "nutcases".

I lead her to the balcony overlooking the arena. In stony silence, we watch the workers making repairs for a few minutes before I start a new conversation. "Most likely, I already know the answer to this question, but still I must ask. What do you think of Lady Scarlett's suggestion that you join the training sessions? Would you consider doing so?"

Surprisingly, she doesn't immediately give me a negative response. After a minute, she sighs. "I suppose I might need to learn how to defend myself in case one of the nobles decides they don't want me around." I'm sure she means Lady Millicent, and I smile as an image flashes through my mind of her being taken down by a Mistem.

"I'll make sure everything you need is provided. I look forward to seeing you at the palace more often," I say in a friendly tone.

Her response is toneless. "I look forward to going home, Your Majesty, which I should probably do before it gets dark." She turns and heads for the door as I glance at the sun, not yet touching the horizon, but getting close. The other guests will likely begin to leave shortly after the fight ends, so I suppose I can indulge her wish.

I catch up to Skylar and fall in stride with her as the doors of the dining hall burst open and Lord Grant storms out sporting a black eye, split lip, and various other gashes and bruises, his red face pointed at the ground in a look of pure fury and humiliation. As he yells for his carriage to be brought out, not noticing us while he heads for the door, General Chase leaves the hall with many new injuries of his own and a triumphant smile. The rest of the guests follow with a chorus of grumbling, gloating, and the clinking of coins as bets are settled. They all pass us with bows, curtseys, and polite expressions of "Good evening, Your Majesty." Some also acknowledge Skylar—Lord Xavier and Lady Millicent doing so using glares that drip with venom.

I accompany Skylar outside where one of my carriages is waiting to take her home. After she climbs into it, I attempt to kiss her hand as I say "goodbye". "I'm certain you'll soon become used to the way things are done here."

"Maybe," she responds, her face blank, then pulls her hand away from me and uses it to slam the carriage door, yanking it from the grasp of a slightly bewildered footman. The carriage pulls away and I quickly turn back into the palace, heading straight for my study to find out how soon I can have an excuse to bring her here again.

19

Ideas and Rivalries

Skylar

For the next few weeks, I'm at the palace more than at home. King Roland seems to send me invitations every other day for court meetings, social gatherings, and training sessions. I want to reject some of them, but my family is still scared. For their sakes, I reply to every message he sends with "yes". It's the one comfort I can give them, now that I'm going berry picking again. I convinced my parents that we need the money. Between that and my palace activities, I barely get to spend time at home.

Of course, the signet ring King Roland gave me remains a secret. I've buried it in the pile of books beside my bed, so the only people who have seen it are myself and the king. He still insists on giving me the noble's salary, but the extra money can be conveniently hidden by the fact that our stand became considerably more popular when word got out about my palace excursions. I often need to deliver freshly picked arda berries in the middle of the day just to keep up with demand, so I slip a little of my money into our cash box while Dad is distracted. I can't hide everything this way, so much of the extra is spent on books and the rest is stowed away with the ring. No one questions it, since we all share any extra money to spend as we please. That means Mandy's happily covering all her clothes in embroidery and my growing book collection doesn't raise suspicion.

Today I'm at the palace arena, surrounded by Haeltons. King Roland was true to his word and made sure that a full suit of fine leather training armour was waiting for me in the guest room I now know so well. Only my white hair distinguishes me from the Haeltons as I dart around a marked-off circle, wielding a heavy wooden sword in a duel with Lady Lauretta.

"Will you stop dodging?" she asks through a half-laugh. The Haeltons constantly tease me for my 'Mistem-ish' form of fighting, using my quicker reflexes to my advantage and dodging their blows before catching them off-guard with my own slashes. My opponent usually complains. "I can't get a hit with you dancing around like that!"

"That's the idea!" I counter. I don't mind dueling with Lady Lauretta. We make it fun by teasing and joking with each other. Lady Clara and Lord Maverick are alright too—I've learned a lot from talking to them—but the way they analyze the duel out loud when they fight, sometimes forgetting what they're doing, can be annoying. Everyone else is a different story.

I laugh and duck away from one of Lauretta's powerful slashes and the force of it throws her off, causing her to stumble. I stay where I am and wait for her to recover, which proves to be a mistake. A burst of stars flashes in front of my eyes as something heavy collides with the back of my head. My sword and the blunt practice javelin clatter to the ground with me. As soon as my head stops swimming enough to stand, I'm on my feet, looking for the javelin thrower. To no surprise, Lady Millicent stands behind me in mock apology.

"Sorry, Mistem. My aim's a bit off today." I glance behind her to the javelin targets, a row of old shields stuck on short poles that can easily be knocked over, standing almost on the opposite side of the arena from the duelling rings.

Your aim isn't the only thing that's off.

King Roland glances over from the duel he's just won against Lord Mason and I try to ignore him like I'm ignoring the throbbing of my head. Never show pain if you want Haeltons to take you seriously. I look Lady Millicent straight in the eye. I don't want to give her the satisfaction of a fight. "You'd better work on it. I'm sure you don't want to have an accident like that in a real battle." Because the king is watching, she contents herself with giving me a sneer before picking up her weapon and walking away.

Lauretta comes up to me, sword lowered as I pick up mine. "You're alright?" It's as much a statement as it is a question.

"I'm fine."

She shakes her head. "You should have met her challenge. You could have brought her down and ended it."

"Do you really think she would leave me alone just because I beat her in a fist fight?"

Lauretta shrugs. "She'd be more careful about provoking you again."

I roll my eyes. "Right. Besides, she wanted a fight. I'm not going to give it to her."

"So, instead you'll let her think you're weak? A pushover? A coward?"

"No. If she decides to start a fight, I'll defend myself, but I won't throw the first punch." With a sigh, Lauretta lets the topic drop.

* * *

Even before I reach the guest room that now seems to have become *mine,* I know something isn't right. The door has been left slightly ajar and the sound of movement comes from inside. Thinking, hoping, that it's Ann or one of the other servants cleaning up or something, I push it open as calmly as I can manage. It isn't Ann who greets me.

"Hello, Mistem," Lady Millicent sneers, looking at her signet ring rather than me as she twists it around her finger. Like me she's still in her training armour, the arena session having ended just a few minutes ago. How fast did she run to get here before me?

"What do you want?" I ask, crossing my arms and putting as much force into my voice as possible.

"To warn you." She's stopped fiddling with her ring, but she still doesn't look at me.

"About what?"

Now she meets my gaze and her voice instantly shifts from casual to a battering ram. "Maybe you're Roland's favourite right now. I don't know what you did to bewitch him or why he's so obsessed, but it isn't going to last. If you value your safety, you'll get out of here before he comes to his senses."

"And you think he's going to go after you when he gets tired of me?"

A smug grin splits her face. "Of course."

I almost feel sorry for Lady Millicent, with her delusional ambitions doomed to failure. Almost. "You'd be welcome to have him; if he wanted you. Are you really so caught up in your own ideas that you can't see the obvious?"

Lady Millicent's fists clench. "What do you mean?"

"You seem to be the only one who doesn't realize that King Roland wants nothing to do with you. Why don't you just give up before you make a fool of yourself?"

In two rapid strides Lady Millicent leers inches from my face, a fist menacingly pointed at my chin. We're almost the same height, and I meet her level gaze without a hint of fear. "Are you looking for a fight, Mistem?"

"*You* are. I'm just trying to give you some good advice."

"Hmph. You're just like every other Mistem, weak."

"I can handle danger just as well as any of you can."

"Then prove it. If you're strong, show me. Fight me!" With each word her voice rises until she's almost screaming in my face. I don't back down.

"Did you ever consider that there might be other ways to show strength?"

Her scoffing laugh tells me she hasn't. "Like what?"

I can't answer her question, but even though I keep quiet my gaze never falters and my face remains stony.

The corner of Lady Millicent's mouth twitches in a barely concealed smirk. "You know what I think? I think you don't have any place being here. You may have put on a good performance in the arena, but you're as much a coward as any other Mistem."

I draw myself up to my full height and lower my clenched fists to my sides. "Why should I care what a bunch of Haelton war-addicts think?" I ask, throwing her words from the dinner party back at her. She lurches toward me, and I brace to defend myself. Then a knock makes us both freeze and we step away from each other as the door opens.

Ann walks in with a bundle in her arms, her usual cheery smile faltering as she notices the Haelton noble. "I-I'm sorry. I, uh, didn't mean to intrude, or . . . " She trips over her words and her eyes sink to the ground, a habit long abandoned in my presence.

"Don't worry about it, Ann. What were you going to say?" I ask, ignoring Lady Millicent's indignant exclamation when I turn my attention away from her to a servant.

Ann holds the bundle toward me. "King Roland thought you might like to have this."

I open the package to reveal a new gown, a deep green one this time, with sleeves that are little more than thin strips of sheer material that would hang off my shoulder. It even has a pocket like the one I added to my other dress! Maybe the king thought I might like to have more variety in my wardrobe. Or he got bored of seeing me in the same blue dress all the time. Whatever his motives are, his gift seems to have offended Lady Millicent. Her eyes bug out and, after a few sputtered attempts at speaking, she storms out of the room faster than I thought any Haelton could possibly move.

I've avoided a fight for another day, but how long can I keep this up?

20

What Will Work?

Roland

Why must some people be so difficult to understand? Skylar, for instance. She accepts all my invitations, even for events that aren't necessary for politicians to attend, but when she comes, it seems she wants nothing more than to leave. If she doesn't want to be here, why won't she simply reject a few of them and stop giving me false hope? I know I promised not to flirt, but that doesn't mean I have to let her keep hating me. Yet Skylar seems determined to hate almost every Haelton she sees, despite my best efforts. I know she has a reason to hate me, and I've tried everything I can think of to apologise and try to make it up to her. I've tried giving her gifts, giving her status and privilege beyond what most Haeltons can even claim, letting her experience the best that palace life has to offer, even giving her space to do what she wants when she's here, but still she is as cold as when we first met and nothing seems to sway her. What does this girl want? How can I get past her shield of perpetual distaste?

Maybe extending an invitation personally rather than through a piece of paper will help. I certainly hope so. My determination is steadily growing as the carriage draws near to Marshwall. I'm tired of seeing a scowl on Skylar's face nearly every time she looks at me. That is, when she's not trying to pretend I don't exist. That's also becoming annoying.

There's a girl tending to a small garden in front of Skylar's house. For an instant I think it's her. However, when she looks up at the approaching carriage, her grey eyes widen before slamming back to the ground. It must be Skylar's sister. "Good morning," I call through the window as she hastily stands and tucks loose strands of hair back into her ponytail.

"G-good morning, Your Majesty," she returns, dipping into a clumsy curtsey. Her voice is quivering nervously.

The footman hops to the ground and opens the door for me. "I don't believe we've been introduced. You must be Skylar's sister," I say lightly as I climb out.

"Yes, S-Sire, I am." After a tense silence she adds, "M-my name is Mandy."

"It's a pleasure to meet you, Mandy." Her only response is to curtsey again.

"I would like to speak to your sister. Is she here?"

"N-no, Sire, I'm sorry, she isn't." She trembles slightly. "B-but she should be back at any moment," she rushes to add. "I-if you would like, you could wait inside for her. I'm certain my mother and I can provide you with refreshments, or . . . " she trails off, looking at a window with a pleading expression. I glance over, but only catch a glimpse of white hair as a head ducks below the window ledge. Skylar's mother seems even more nervous than her sister, if such a thing is possible. I can see from the corner of my eye that she's watching through the window, but every time my eyes start to wander in that direction she ducks out of sight.

"Thank you for the offer, but that won't be necessary." Mandy's shoulders relax slightly. "Do you know where Skylar is?"

"S-she went to the market, Sire. She should be home any minute."

"Hmm, I wonder what she would be doing there," I think aloud, hoping that some small talk will lighten the mood. Mandy at least stops stuttering.

"She's probably in the bookshop, Sire."

"You think so?"

"Definitely. Skylar goes to that shop every time she's in the market. She loves reading."

"Is that so?" I ask, suddenly interested.

"Yes, Your Majesty. She reads almost every chance she has," Mandy continues eagerly, seeming to note my interest.

"Any type in particular?"

"Oh, she reads all sorts of books, though she mostly likes ones with what she calls 'exciting stories' in them."

I smile my thanks, an idea quickly forming in my head, as the sound of footsteps on the road draws nearer.

21

AAAAAAGH!

Skylar

As I head home, the one thing that keeps me calm is looking forward to relaxing with a book for the rest of the day. I helped Dad take the especially large load to the market this morning and stopped at the book shop before heading back. Bad decision. Now that people know I'm often at the palace, they stare at me every time I go to the market. I've always had glances shot at me in public, disapproving or confused looks mostly, but this is different. The Haeltons keep gawking and the Mistems have started avoiding my eyes the way they do with Haeltons. I try to find solace in the shelves of books, but even that doesn't always work. Sometimes, like today, I can hardly focus on the titles in front of me. Mark, the shopkeeper, has stopped calling me *Misty*, but he's replaced it with something worse. *My Lady*. Everywhere I go, everyone keeps greeting me with that phrase. No one knows about the ring, but the Mistems probably assume I have a title now, and the Haeltons, out of spite, keep mocking me with it. Every time it's the same thing: *My Lady, My Lady, My Lady.* It's not bad enough that I'm surrounded almost every day by those pompous, war-crazed Haelton snobs who only have a few decent characters among them, but to be considered one of them? If I hear one more person say, 'My Lady', I am going to scream.

"Good morning, My Lady!"

Don't crack in front of the king, don't crack in front of the king. "I have a name, you know," I snap instead.

"Of course, Rose, I just—"

"Still wrong."

With a bemused smile and a roll of his eyes, King Roland humours me. "Alright, Skylar."

I nod stiffly. "Now, what do you want?"

"A civil greeting, perhaps?"

"Then you shouldn't have come to me." King Roland almost laughs at that, but Mandy looks terrified. Her wide eyes glisten as she silently pleads with me to stop mouthing off to the king. I give her an encouraging smile and motion for her to go inside. She refuses, probably to keep an eye on me. I turn back to the king and try to soften my tone slightly for her sake. "What did you really come here for?"

"I was hoping you would accompany me to the palace."

"You couldn't have just sent an invitation?"

"I could have, but I wanted to come in person. There's something I want to show you."

I glance over at Mandy and my mom's face peeking through the window. So much for relaxing. "Fine, just let me get ready."

"Certainly," he responds as Mandy scoots into the house and I quickly follow.

*   *   *

The sound of my green skirt swishing across the marble floor is the only thing that breaks the silence as the king leads me through the castle. I've never been in this area before. There aren't any suits of armour or portraits displayed here, like in most of the other halls. Instead the walls are lined with paintings and tapestries depicting scenes from stories, most of them fight scenes. I recognize some of them from my books, but most are unfamiliar. One tapestry catches my eye and I stop to examine it while King Roland keeps walking, apparently not paying attention to me. The tapestry shows two armies facing off, two straight lines of armoured figures glowing in the sun shining on a misty field which is about to become a battle ground.

"Are you coming, Skylar?" King Roland asks, realizing I've stopped.

"Where exactly are we going?"

"You will see when we get there," he answers vaguely.

"Why don't you just tell me?"

"I want it to be a surprise," he states over his shoulder as he keeps walking. I'm not sure I want to see another of the king's *surprises*, but all I can do is follow.

I catch up to him in front of two giant oak doors. He pauses, turning to me with a barely concealed grin. "Ready to see this?"

"Considering I don't know what 'this' is..."

The king's grin widens as he turns the knob. "Don't worry, I promise you'll like it." He stands back as he opens the door, letting me enter the room first.

I'm glad the king can't see my face as my jaws drop and I have to stifle a gasp. Books. I'm surrounded by books. Of course, a palace like this would have a huge library, but I didn't expect this. The two-story-high walls are covered by full bookshelves. A platform runs the length of the room halfway up and ladders are dotted around, providing access to books too high to reach. You could fit four bookstores in here, maybe even more! I think of the pile of books I have at home and wonder how I could ever have called that a big collection. This is like a dream come true!

"Come this way." There's a smile in the king's voice, but I don't want to look at him and betray my excitement. Still staring at the shelves, I follow the sound of King Roland's footsteps. "Here's a section you might enjoy," he says, stopping in front of a line of shelves. "There's quite a lot of action in these stories."

Finally getting my facial expressions under control and turning to him with a stare that's as blank as I can make it, I demand, "What makes you think I would like any of this?"

The king replies with a smirk, "I heard it from a reliable source."

"Sure," I say, rolling my eyes. "What 'source' told you that?"

"Your sister."

That miserable traitor.

King Roland scans the shelves, then takes down a book and hands it to me. "I think you'll enjoy this one. It's where the scene from the tapestry you were admiring was taken." Oh, so he was paying attention.

The king turns his back to me, browsing the titles to select a book for himself, and I sneak away. Running silently, I find a staircase to the second level and climb it, searching the balcony for a hidden spot. I find a window that's blocked from view by bookcases on either side. It juts out to overlook the garden, the wide ledge covered by cushions. Perfect. I open the book as I sit down and immediately begin devouring the pages, absorbing the story with relish. Maybe King Roland has finally given me something I really like, but that doesn't mean I have to be anywhere near him to enjoy it.

* * *

My fingers drum along the cover of the book the way they often do at an exciting part. I'm completely lost in the story, in the suspense, the struggle, the building battle. So much so that I lose track of where I am and don't hear the approaching footsteps. Not until I'm rudely pulled back to the real world by his voice. "You really are good at hiding." I sigh as the king sits down and I move as far away from him as the window seat will allow.

"When I hide it means I don't want to be seen. By *anyone*."

"Don't you think your host would want to talk to you?"

"I don't know why my host even wants to be my host."

"What do you mean?"

I look the king straight in the eyes, all the pent-up frustrations of the past months rushing back to me, begging to be released. "I mean why did you bring me here? Not just today, but when you first saw me. Why didn't you simply keep going? Why did you look for me after I left the first time? Why do you keep inviting me back here? You know I only come because I want to help my people, but so far, I'm the only Mistem who's been affected. There hasn't been so much as a suggestion to stop the collections or anything because I never get the chance to mention it. All you Haeltons want to do is talk about the war and ignore my suggestions to just make a deal with Mishfont and end it. So, what's the point of having me here?"

"I've already told you, to keep pea—"

"To keep peace within Respenda? To make the common people believe you care about them because you listen to a Mistem? We both know that's a lie. If all you cared about was appearances, you might let people see me in the palace once in a while, but you wouldn't keep trying to make me like you. You would have given up on that idea long ago, no matter how stubborn and competitive Haeltons can be. For once, could you take a break from acting like a king, stop giving me the political excuses, and just tell me the real reason?"

"You don't think the political reasons *are* my only reasons? That what I care about most is my country?" There's the slightest waver in his voice, as if his confidence is just starting to break.

"I think you can stop trying to copy your parents, or whatever overlord you're emulating all the time to prove you can run a country. You don't need to keep making the same mistakes they did to earn people's confidence. It doesn't always work."

Apparently, something I've said impacts King Roland. He freezes, staring past me with unseeing eyes. He doesn't even blink when I wave my hand in front of his face. Did I just break the king? Maybe it's best if I go somewhere else.

I hold up the book in my hand to see if he'll respond. "Could I take this to the garden?" The king gives an almost imperceptible nod and I rush out of the library before he comes to his senses.

22

History

Roland

I sit frozen for what seems like hours, trying to push back the past fighting its way into my mind. It's a fruitless effort. Skylar's words keep bringing it back.

She mentioned my parents' 'mistakes', the way they ruled Respenda, and said it didn't work. Does she realize what she said? Can I tell her?

I finally settle the debate in my head and turn to Skylar. *Oh, right. She went outside.* I head out to the garden and find Skylar on a bench near a rose bush, once again absorbed in the book I gave her. I smile inwardly, this little triumph softening my hesitation at what I'm about to say. She glances up as I sit down, closing the book with her finger marking the page.

She forgoes any greeting. "What exactly did I say that was so shocking?"

"You made me remember something I don't usually think about."

"And?"

"I thought about it."

"And?"

"You're right. I do want to see you for more selfish reasons than I let on." I pause for a moment to let her respond and give myself time to think. Skylar only stares at me, expectant, waiting for me to continue.

"Did you come to tell me why or just to admit I'm right?"

I take a breath before I speak. "You know how my parents died?"

"Sort of. In the villages we just heard that there was some sort of accident."

Great. I must go through the whole story. Already, unsettling images from the past flood my mind. "It was not an accident. It was simply meant to look like one."

"Then, what did happen?" Skylar curiously raises her brows.

"They had just left for a political visit to another city. Originally all three of us were meant to go, but at the last minute my parents decided that I would stay here. The Mishfont spies and the traitors who helped them didn't know that."

Pity seems to bloom in Skylar's eyes as the reality dawns on her. "Sabotage?"

I nod. "They managed to loosen a wheel on the carriage before my parents left. It came off as they were passing the marshes."

"Oh," is all she says, looking away.

"They were hurt in the crash, but not fatally. Just enough that they weren't able to get away."

Skylar's fingers brush the scars on her arm, and she winces. "The knightcrawlers?"

I glance at her arm, the three long, red stripes detailing the damage that those beasts can do in only a second, if given a chance to grab hold. "Yes." There's a pause as I relive that day in my head. The messenger running into the palace, hearing the whispered conversations with the counsel before I'm given the dreadful news. "The counsel didn't want me there when my parents' bodies were brought in. They didn't think great warriors should be remembered in light of a defeat like that. But I wanted to see them, to see for myself if all they told me was true. I snuck down as the corpses were carried in and regretted doing so as soon as I saw them." I think back to when Skylar was first in the arena, watching again from afar as the claws of a knightcrawler nearly tore her arm off. Given the state my parents were in, I can only imagine what those creatures did. "Such attacks can leave a person almost unrecognisable."

"I can imagine," Skylar responds, covering her scars with her hand. "That must have been really hard." I nod, not trusting myself to say anything. She takes a breath and opens her mouth, then closes it again. I wait in silence until she speaks. "That's why you set knightcrawlers on the people who spoke against you? To give traitors a taste of what they did to your parents?"

I shake my head. "The ones who caused their deaths were caught and dealt with years ago. I just thought it would be a good deterrent for anyone else who might cause trouble."

"Or it would make them hate you more and try to get the tyrant off the throne."

A faint smile comes to my lips. "Or that."

"You still haven't explained what that has to do with bringing a Mistem to the palace and making her a Lady."

"You can't tell anyone this . . . " I wait until she nods before continuing, "but to this day I still have trouble looking at the marshes whenever I go past them. I've tried to hide and overcome this fear ever since they were killed, to no avail."

"Why should it matter?" Skylar says, scowling. "I mean, of course I used to think that Haelton's weren't bothered by anything, but now I know you have problems just like every other normal person. It's understandable."

"That's the issue! We aren't supposed to let anyone know we have problems. A king especially should never show weakness of any kind, no matter how understandable it is!" My voice is rising with the heat in my face. I take a breath to calm myself before speaking again. "That's why I wanted you around. I looked into the marshes that day for the first time in years to see a Mistem girl leaping among the trees as if there was nothing to fear. After what I saw from you, in the marshes and the arena, I almost thought you were incapable of being scared. I thought if you were near me enough, maybe some of that quality would rub off on me."

"Is that still the case? All you want from me is bravery lessons?"

"Not really," I reply with a smirk. "Now it's simply dull around here when you're gone."

"Oh, what, so I'm just some type of entertainment?!" she raises her voice a little, trying to turn a smile into a scowl.

I grin back. "No, you're something special, R—"

"DON'T!" she shouts, deftly grabbing a rose from the bush and brandishing the thorny stem towards my face. "Don't you dare."

" . . . Skylar," I correct myself, grin widening.

She settles back, fingering the petals on the flower. "I'll admit that my life has certainly been more interesting in the past couple of months."

We sit back for a few minutes, contently watching the sun setting. Then we realize the sun is setting.

"I need to go," Skylar says quickly, standing up and holding the book out to me.

I push her hand back towards her. "You can keep it until you're done reading it."

She smiles her thanks. "You'll probably have it back in a day or two, then."

"Well, feel free to raid the library any time you want."

She holds her hands up in mock reluctance. "Don't tempt me! You won't have anything left for yourself."

I grin and take one of her hands. She flinches but doesn't pull away this time when I kiss it in a regal farewell. "Good night, Skylar."

"Good night, Roland." She flashes a smile and disappears down the garden path.

23

Marshes

Skylar

M y breath hisses from my teeth in a half-growl, half-sigh as a mucky, wet feeling soaks through my clothes. I put down my half-filled berry basket and my spear as I try pull my legs out of the muddy patch I slipped in. On firmer ground, I survey the damage and grumble again at the slimy, mud-brown stains covering my clothes up to the knees. I don't mind the feeling of wearing dirty clothes, but I've been pretty careless about keeping them clean since I don't have to hide evidence of my marsh excursions anymore, and Mom said that the next time I came home with slime-covered clothes I'd have to wash them myself. This stuff is a pain to clean.

Since there's nothing I can do about it now, I'll try and gather enough arda berries for dessert tonight and hopefully put Mom in a good mood. I'm taking aim at a large clump of them when a twig snaps behind me. I whip around, pointing my spear at the intruder instead.

"I come in peace!" Roland proclaims with raised hands and a toothy smile.

"You know, if you want to avoid injury it might be a good idea not to sneak up on an armed person in places like this," I remark as I lower the spear.

"Probably," he shrugs, but his eyes dart nervously through the trees. "But I have my own protection against such misunderstandings." He rests a hand on the sword sheathed at his hip. The weapon is definitely good enough to stop a hastily thrown stick, but are his reflexes?

"I take it that's the only protection you have with you?" I ask, noticing the lack of guards in the area. I don't even see signs of a carriage or a driver. "How did you get here?"

"I walked over." He chuckles when I raise an eyebrow. "There was no pressing business at the palace today, so I thought I would take a break and see how common people live. See if I could blend in."

"You're doing a terrible job," I remark, scanning the fine clothes he's wearing. The deep red suit isn't like his royal outfits and is probably less expensive than what he usually wears, but it's still a lot nicer than anything *common people* can afford.

"Oh well," he sighs. "I mainly wanted to visit you at your house, and I thought your family would find me less threatening if I came alone. Then I heard you splashing around in here while passing by," he pointedly glances at my stained clothes, "and I decided to make a detour."

"Just for me? How touching!" I say in a sarcastic, gushing tone. "But I'm afraid I don't have much time for talking at the moment. I'm working." I point to my basket on the ground and turn to take aim at the berries again.

"I can help you with that," Roland offers, stepping beside me.

"Are you sure?" I ask. "How much berry picking experience do you have?"

"Oh, it can't be too hard. Watch. You want those ones?" he points to the clump I was aiming at. "I'll get them for you." Before I can protest, he strides over to the tree beside us, which has a leafless branch extending towards the berries, and begins climbing.

"I wouldn't do that, if I were you," I warn.

"Why? You think Mistems are the only good climbers?" He isn't looking at me as he inches out on the branch, reaching for his sword and preparing to cut down the berries.

"No, I mean that branch is—" CRACK! SPLOOSH! "— dead."

As Roland rises from the water, spluttering, muttering, and trying to wipe the muck off his face, I quickly cover my mouth to hold back the shriek of laughter threatening to escape.

"Don't . . . say . . . a word . . . about this," he grinds out.

"Sure," I agree, my voice shaking with suppressed giggles. I look away from his scowling face to quickly bring down the offending fruit, letting both berries and spear land just behind Roland. He retrieves them for me, then pops a berry in his mouth as he wades back. "Hey!" I grab the berries from his hand and put them in the basket before he can take any more. "You're eating my family's income."

"Why do you need it? You make enough on your own now," he remarks as he hands me my spear. I turn away, pretending to inspect the arda berries. Apparently, that's the only answer he needs. "Your family doesn't know about that, do they?"

I turn to face him, making my expression and tone as neutral as possible. "What makes you think that?"

Roland points to my bare right hand with his own adorned one, the signet ring shining through a thin layer of grime. "You never wear the ring, you cringe every time someone calls you 'Lady', you try to hide every time you're in a carriage going to or from the palace; you constantly try to deny that we ever had that conversation. I thought you would at least tell your family, but if they still don't know that you make more than enough to support them without the berry business, I suppose I was wrong."

I look down, suddenly feeling ashamed, without knowing why. Because I'm keeping secrets from my family again? No, I never felt guilty about that before. I was doing it to help all of us. Why should this be different? It isn't dangerous, and the only thing that would change if they knew would be Mom and Dad wanting new things for the house and Mandy begging me to take her to raid some of the shops. So why should I feel guilty now? I lift my gaze to Roland's sun-yellow eyes. "My family is fine with the way things are and they don't need to know about this. It shouldn't matter whether I want to be treated like a noble or not."

"What's wrong with being treated like a noble?" I can't answer, but Roland seems to know anyway. "You don't want people to associate you with us?"

"No, I don't." I have to be honest. Roland's lips purse, quizzical, but also hurt.

"I can understand your aversion to some of the others; I don't like many of them myself." I smile weakly at that. "But to hate the very idea of being associated with anyone who has a title? What's causing that?" I shrug, kind of knowing the answer but not wanting to say it out loud. Roland has no such hesitation. "It's me, isn't it?" he almost whispers. "You haven't forgiven me for the arena incidents and don't want to have anything that connects you with me."

For a moment, I can't say anything. When I do speak, my voice is low and hesitant. "I told you before, actions like that are hard to forgive. Really hard. I should think you, of all people, would know that." I look straight into his eyes and my tone becomes accusatory. "Have you forgiven Mishfont? Are you going to keep handling *traitors* the way you did the ones I helped? Are you still seeking some form of revenge?"

It's Roland's turn to look away. "That's different," he mutters. "You and your father survived. And Mishfont hasn't tried to make amends for what they did."

He has a point. But still, something holds me back. Memories from when I was a child flood my mind. Watching other Mistems cower as they were forced to sell their wares for next to nothing, Dad pulling me into some hidden crevice when guards came to collect, and always, always, being told the same thing: *keep your head down; it's the safest way to live.* "It's hard to change a mindset you've always had," I tell Roland. He nods, understanding.

We stand in silence until we're both startled out of our musings by a splash a few yards away. A knightcrawler has appeared, lounging on a rock a short distance from us. It's far enough, though, that it doesn't seem to have noticed us yet. I glance over at Roland, not surprised to see his face blanche. But he quickly shoves his fear behind a wall of anger and reaches for his sword. I grab his hand and mouth "Don't!" but it's too late. Roland has already partially drawn his sword, and the sound of the metal sliding against the sheath draws the knightcrawler's attention. It turns towards us, its tongue flicking once before it slides into the water and heads straight for our little island.

In seconds, Roland's blade is free of its sheath, my spear is ready to thrust at the oncoming menace, and said menace is lunging out of the water at us. Roland steps in front of me, sword flashing as the sharp end slices through the air toward the beast's neck. "No!" I shout, bumping his arm so that the blunt side of the blade collides with the lizard's head instead. It falls, dazed, in front of me, but quickly recovers. It lunges at me with a venomous hiss. I thrust the butt of my spear directly into its open mouth, knocking it against the back of its throat. It falls back, shaking its scaly head. From the ground it takes a wild swipe. It nearly catches Roland's arm as he knocks its skull with the hilt of his sword. As a final blow, Roland kicks the knightcrawler's head away from us, sending the beast sprawling. It lies senseless on the ground with half its body in the water.

I pick up my basket and grab his arm. When he drags his gaze away from our unconscious adversary, I motion that we should leave, and he follows me to another grove of arda trees, far from the knightcrawler.

"What was that about?" Roland demands when we've gone far enough that we can't see the beast anymore.

"What do you mean?"

He rolls his eyes, as if it should be obvious. "I mean, why were you so intent on sparing the knightcrawler? It would have been better to kill the thing."

"You think it's better to kill a creature that's just looking for food? That's trying to survive?" I counter, a bit smug.

Roland lets out an exasperated sigh. "We're trying to survive, too, and things like that would kill us without a second thought."

"Yes, but they *can't* think the way we do. They just focus on their own survival, while we're capable of thinking about more than ourselves." I turn away and resume berry picking.

Shaking his head, Roland helps me. This time he stays on the ground and cuts down lower bunches of fruit with his sword. "Is that how all Mistems deal with danger? *Don't hurt the adversary because they have their own motives?*"

"No," I reply from where I pick up a freshly cut cluster of berries. "Most would just run away. Or, no, actually they probably wouldn't be in a place like this at all."

"Most likely not," Roland laughs, catching some berries as they fall and placing them in the basket. After a few minutes of silent gathering, he speaks again. "You really have interesting views on fighting."

"So I've been told," I reply. "Many, many times." Roland laughs again.

When the basket is full, I pick it up as Roland sheaths his sword. He wipes the sweat from his brow, flicks a glob of—something—off his sleeve, then removes the jacket he was wearing. The cream-coloured shirt underneath is wet, but the jacket protected if from marsh muck. It's now harder to tell that he fell into the murky water.

"Thanks for your help," I tell him, and I realize that this is probably the first time he's done anything resembling real work.

"It's no trouble." He tucks his jacket under his arm and walks beside me along the trail leading home.

24

Good News and Bad News

Skylar

Roland walks with me all the way to my house. Along the trail we make polite conversation, but neither of us brings up the topic we were discussing before the knightcrawler interrupted us. When we come in sight of the house, I slow my pace, realizing that for the first time I want to keep talking with Vexenta's king. Roland slows too.

"Would you like to come in?" I ask, trying to sound casual.

Roland smiles past a grimace. "I'd like to, but I don't want to cause any of your family members to have a nervous breakdown."

I force a laugh. "Just let me go in first and warn them, then it should be alright." I leave him standing along the wall near the door. I leave it open and stand just inside so that he can hear the conversation.

"Skylar . . . ." Mom says, glaring at my stained clothes as I place the berry basket on the counter beside her. Mandy looks over from the mixing bowl and rolls her eyes.

"I know, I know," I respond while returning my spear to its new spot beside the door. "I'll wash these myself later."

"That didn't take long," Dad remarks from the table where he's counting this week's profits, a steaming cup of coffee sitting beside him. Mom and Mandy are having trouble keeping up with the demand for our products, and they didn't have enough goods baked for Dad to sell today, so he decided to do some work at home.

"Well, I did have a bit of help." Everyone pauses and looks at me, waiting for more. "Roland stopped by while I was in the marshes and gave me a hand." They exchange surprised looks, but no one questions my statement.

"I take it that means you'll be going to the palace today?" Dad asks, taking a sip of his coffee.

"No, actually. I was, um, wondering if it would be alright if he came in here." The reaction is immediate. Mom drops her rolling pin with a loud *clunk* onto the counter, Mandy squeals and both her hands shoot up to cover her mouth, and Dad has a coughing fit as he nearly chokes on his drink. I look out the door at Roland, who smiles resignedly and tries not to laugh.

Mandy is the first to recover enough to speak. "Please tell me you're joking. I mean . . . he's . . . with what . . . and I can't let a king see me like this!" she gestures to her flour-covered apron and hands.

"Why would I joke about that? I know what you're trying to say, but trust me, I wouldn't let him in here if I thought he'd put anyone in danger. Also, it doesn't really matter how you look. Do you think I'm worried?" I point to my own mud-stained legs.

"Well, sorry for caring about appearances," she retorts, hands on her hips. "Tell me we at least have a little time to get ready first."

"Considering he's right outside . . . " I say, motioning to the open door. With another squeal, Mandy rushes into our bedroom, slamming the door shut behind her.

I look to Mom and Dad, who are now hurriedly cleaning up the money box and baking supplies. "If you need more warning before having visitors, I can ask Roland to come back another—"

"No, it's alright." Dad says, stashing away the cashbox in the bedroom he and Mom share. "If the king is already here, we can do our best with what we have. But Skylar . . . " Dad motions for me to come to him and I step over to the table. "Are you sure about this?" he whispers. "After all that's happened, is it really safe?"

"You're the ones who have been convincing me to go to the palace for the past two months, despite what happened there and the fact that I didn't want to go. Was that safe?"

Dad looks away. "We didn't want you to go, but keeping the king happy seemed safer than having him come break down our door. And he acts—differently—around you. It didn't seem like you were in danger. But you're sure about bringing him in here?"

"Trust me. We've come to an—understanding—and he really seems to regret the arena incidents. Both of them."

Dad raises his brows sceptically, but he nods to me. "Fine."

Now doubting whether this was a good idea, I motion for Roland to come in. He enters with a smile plastered on his face. If he hopes to diffuse some tension, it doesn't work very well. To avoid an awkward silence, I make introductions.

"Roland, this is my mother," I say, gesturing to Mom, who's just pulled fresh pastries from the oven and is now making drinks to serve our guest. She drops what she's doing and dips into a curtsey.

"Y-your Majesty," she says, her voice so low we can hardly hear it.

Roland dips his head in greeting. "It's a pleasure to meet you."

I turn to Dad next. "You've already met my father." I try to make my voice sound light and casual, hoping we can pass over the nature of that first meeting. It doesn't work.

"Yes, and I believe I should apologize for my actions that day," Roland states. The sincerity of his tone and soft expression startle both my parents.

"I-it's no matter," Dad mutters, bowing, probably more as an excuse not to make eye contact than as a show of respect.

"No, really," Roland insists. "I was being irrational, and it was wrong of me. I hope that someday I can make amends." Stunned, Dad doesn't respond. He and Mom just keep exchanging looks, letting the awkward silence stretch out.

I'm not sure how to get my parents to relax. Fortunately, Mandy comes to my rescue before the silence lasts for too long. She emerges from our room with her hair neatly pinned away from her face, wearing her best dress, which is heavily embroidered with a flowery pattern around the edges. At least I can keep the conversation going a little longer.

"I take it you've also met Mandy before," I say as my sister curtseys.

"Indeed, I have. It's wonderful to see you again, Mandy." Roland nods regally as Mandy, who hasn't straitened up yet, smiles at the ground.

"It's an honour, Your Majesty," she replies.

"That's a lovely dress you're wearing," he comments.

Mandy blushes. "Oh, thank you, Sire."

"The embroidery is exquisite," he continues.

Mandy doesn't reply, but I see what Roland's doing and I immediately seize the opportunity. "She did it herself," I tell him.

He smiles at me before turning back to Mandy. "You are quite talented."

Mandy beams, but doesn't look up. "Thank you, Sire."

Somehow that compliment, as small as it is, deflates some of the tension in the air. Everyone breathes a sigh of relief and relax slightly, finally deciding that Roland isn't such a danger anymore.

"Please, have a seat," Mom says, motioning towards the table. Roland sits down first and the rest of us follow suit. I sit beside Roland while Dad and Mandy settle themselves across the table from us. Mom brings over a tray of drinks and pastries before sitting down beside Dad. The conversation that follows is mostly pleasant small talk. Roland compliments Mom and Mandy's baking, Dad talks about business in the market, and Roland and I joke about the time we had berry picking. I don't mention the incident with the dead branch, but Roland scowls playfully when I look pointedly at his jacket, which is now hanging over the back of his chair, inside-out, to hide the dirt. Then Mandy brings up a very different topic.

"Skylar tells us a lot about the palace and the Haelton courtiers," she remarks.

"Only because you all keep asking for every detail I can give," I retort.

"Because it's something different that no one else we know can talk about. Of course, we want to know details!"

"Girls, please!" Mom scolds, glancing at Roland. Apparently, she doesn't realize that he's used to watching people squabble.

Roland just waves it off with a good-natured smile. "Don't worry about it." He looks over at Mandy. "If you want to know about your sister's experiences at the palace, I can tell you she's quite popular among the nobles."

"I don't know how you define 'popular' . . . " I mutter.

He grins at me. "They notice you."

"It's a little hard not to," I point out, pulling at a strand of my stark-white hair and glancing at the golden features he shares with all the other Haeltons.

"Maybe," he shrugs. "But you also attract attention with your new ideas. Oh, and that reminds me of something I was meaning to tell you."

He has my family's undivided attention. I frown at him, meandering between curiosity and suspicion. "What is it?"

Roland grins widely, looking as if he could burst. "You don't need to worry about collections anymore."

Roland's excitement is met with stunned silence from all around the table. I'm the first to get my voice back. "Do you mean just us or everyone?"

His grin widens. "Everyone," he answers. Again, silence. We can hardly believe what we're hearing. After all these years of Mistems hiding while all they have to live off of is forcibly taken from them, are the collections really going to stop? Just like that? Seeing our disbelief, Roland continues. "The army is funded well enough by what the country produces without taking up the soldiers' time collecting, and so I didn't think it was necessary to continue with that. Besides," he gazes at me, "it seemed like the right course of action."

The shocked expressions around the table slowly morph into smiles that mirror Roland's. I sense Mom and Dad's hands clasping under the table as they face each other with ecstatic grins, but Mandy's eyes dart between me and Roland. "Did Skylar help with that decision?"

Roland doesn't take his eyes off me. "I'd never have thought about it if it weren't for her."

My eyes dart away, but I catch a sly look from Mandy that I'm not sure I like. I turn back to Roland, my face breaking into a wide smile that says everything before my mouth can. "That's great, Roland. That really is fantastic."

Soon we're all happily chatting on and on about this new law, speculating on how everyone will react and how things will change because of it. Until the clatter of a carriage and a loud knock at the door interrupts us.

Dad quickly gets up to answer it. He's about to say something when he opens the door, but he stops and instead stands aside to reveal a Haelton in a palace uniform. Roland immediately gets up and heads over to him while Dad returns to the table, barely noticed.

"What is it?" Roland demands.

"Sire," he responds, bowing. "An urgent report came in at the palace." The messenger holds out a piece of paper to Roland, who grabs it and reads quickly. We all watch his face, which becomes ever darker as his eyes skim along the lines running down the page.

When he finishes, he turns to the messenger, looking again like a military leader. "Send messages to the council. Call a meeting immediately."

"Yes, Sire," he responds, turning on his heel and hopping on a horse standing nearby. He gallops past the carriage which has come to fetch Roland.

Roland turns back to us, striding to the table and grabbing his jacket. "I'm sorry to cut our visit short, but I need to go," he says in a rush.

I stand up as he starts to leave. "Should I come too?"

Roland hesitates, looking between me and the paper in his hand. "You might want to," he finally says.

I nod and dash into my room. I can change at the palace, so all I need to do is grab my blue gown. I don't know what makes me do this, but as an afterthought I dig through my pile of books, pull my signet ring from among the hidden coin purses, and shove it into my pocket. My arms laden with fabric, I head for the door. "I'll be back as soon as possible," I promise my family as I pass them. They're all stuck at the table, held there by worry at the sudden problem arising.

Roland and I quickly climb into the waiting carriage. It starts to move immediately, even as the footman is climbing back into his seat, and rapidly picks up speed. I look at Roland, sitting with his head in one hand, the elbow resting on his knee. The other hand holds the paper in front of his eyes as he rereads it.

"Roland?" He looks up. "What's going on? What does the message say?"

With a sigh, Roland sits up, gazing in my general direction but not making eye contact as he answers. "Mishfont is mobilizing its army and is heading for the borders near Respenda. It seems we have a battle on our hands."

25

Brewing Battle

Skylar

Roland waits by the entrance to the throne room when I arrive. He's back in elaborate royal garb, with the crown of swords on his head and an ornamental sword sheathed at his side. The sound of dozens of voices all talking at once drifts through the closed doors. When he sees me coming, Roland nods in greeting and turns to tell the guards to open the doors, but I stop him.

"Do you really think fighting is the only way to deal with this?"

"Do you have another idea?"

"Yes."

Roland pauses for a moment, a smirk playing at the corners of his mouth. "Okay, but I don't think we have time to try your type of ideas."

Before I can respond, the doors open and Roland strides to the throne at the front of the room. I slip over to my regular seat along the side while everyone stands at the king's entry. When he reaches the dais, he motions for all of us to sit, although he remains standing, pacing a little as he speaks.

"As you have all heard, Mishfont is quickly mobilizing their army, gathering more forces from their outposts as they go, and making to cross the border that will bring them closest to our capital. They could be here in a week, maybe two or three, but we won't have so much as a month to prepare. We need an effective plan that can be quickly executed."

Finished with his speech, Roland sits, resting one hand on the arm of his throne and scanning the room. All around us the nobles are muttering, brainstorming ideas to keep the advancing army out of our country. Lady Clara stands, and the room falls silent as she addresses the king.

"Your Majesty, if we were to cut them off just beyond the eastern hills there is less chance that they'll see us coming and we'll have the advantage of higher ground. It won't matter then if we don't have time to gather the numbers that Mishfont has."

Lord Xavier jumps up from his seat. "But that doesn't mean numbers will be insignificant! We'll be slaughtered if we don't have at least enough soldiers to surround those hills!"

"I have to agree," Roland responds, nodding at him. "General Chase!" he calls. The general shoots up from his seat while Lady Clara and Lord Xavier sit down again. "How many can you have gathered at the hills in a week?"

"Everyone in the eastern outposts and all the soldiers that can be spared from the forts to the north and south, Your Majesty," he answers.

"Attain soldiers from every post that the message can reach in time," Roland commands. General Chase nods and sits as Roland calls on Lord Declan. "How many fighters can you have armed by then?"

"As many as the general can provide," he states.

"See to it," Roland tells him. When Lord Declan is back in his chair, Roland rises from the throne, sword and crown flashing as he paces, his gaze taking in the whole room. "If we do this right, we could not only keep Mishfont away from our country but perhaps also make headway into their territory. I'm confident in the strength of Vexenta and in our soldiers. And, of course, in all of you." Roland's eyes sweep the room. "I'm calling on every noble in fighting condition to be at the head of the army. I will lead the charge myself. We can win this battle, and we can win the war!"

Murmurs of approval and agreement ripple through the crowd. I wait until the sound ebbs. "And how many will die in the attempt?"

Suffocating silence fills the room. "What?" Lord Maverick asks, quiet, but his voice echoes off the stone walls.

"Please tell me this isn't going to be another of your 'peace and treaty' speeches, Lady Skylar," Lady Millicent complains.

I look her straight in the eye as I stand. "I'm not going to lie, Lady Millicent." A collective groan resounds. Only Roland doesn't join in, his gaze meeting mine with a resigned shake of his head.

"We don't have time for this!" Lord Mason shouts.

"Mishfont's king won't listen to talks of peace!" Lord Grant adds.

"Then we make him listen. We take away his biggest support, destabilize his army from the inside, until my 'ridiculous suggestion' becomes the best option he has."

The murmuring becomes a roar of disagreement that seems to make the air vibrate until Roland silences everyone with a raised hand. Then he turns to me. "How would you suggest we do that?" He doesn't sound confident, but it gives me an opportunity, and I rush to seize it.

"By allying with their Mistem soldiers." My statement is met with dead silence, and I brace myself for the coming explosion. Soon shouts are bouncing off the walls all around me.

"That's insane!"

"What could they do?!"

"Are you serious?"

"Enough!" Roland's yell brings instant quiet. He glares around the room, daring anyone to restart the barrage of shouting.

Calmly, Lady Lauretta stands and looks over to me. "Lady Skylar, I must ask, how could that plan help? The Mistems aren't likely to listen to us, and if Mishfont commanders found out what we were doing, which would be extremely obvious if a Haelton were seen frequently talking to Mistems, any spies we sent would never make it back."

"I know. That's why someone should go who can blend in with the Mistems. Someone they won't notice or care about whom the Mistems are more likely to trust."

"Are you suggesting yourself?" Roland's stern tone indicates that he'll never allow it, but I need to try.

"Yes. If a Mistem goes to talk to Mistems, they're more likely to listen. The Haelton commanders will hardly care about seeing another pale face walking around and likely won't pay attention. The Mistems are probably already on the verge of rebellion or desertion since they've been forced to fight; we may just need to give them a little push in the direction we want, and they can weaken Mishfont's army from the inside."

Roland shakes his head. Before I can protest, he raises his hand to keep me quiet. "It's too risky. We'll stick with the battle plan we have." With all argument cut off, I sit down and let the continuing strategy discussions wash over me, unheard.

* * *

When the meeting ends, I'm out the door before everyone else can even leave their seats. I don't look back or slow my stride, even as the sound of hurried footsteps and a faint metallic tapping draws closer. I don't stop until Roland's hand on my shoulder gives me few other options.

"You're angry with me, aren't you?" he asks, spinning me around to face him.

"Why would you think *that*, Your Majesty?" I spit back.

Roland's face softens, pleading. "I did what was necessary. We're familiar with battle, we know what to expect and how to handle it. We don't know how your plan could turn out. I don't want to take that chance. Especially not with you." He holds my gaze, and I pause before responding.

"I know. You made the choice you've been raised to make, and I won't be able to change your mind."

"Skylar . . . "

"No, you've made your decision. If you think facing a charging army head-on holds less risk than weakening it from the inside, fine. I guess we'll just have to wait and see how this ends."

"You don't have to come if you don't want to fight."

"I thought you said you were counting on everyone in fighting condition to help."

"Yes, but I can make an exception. No one will complain. Besides," he smirks, "didn't you say it's a bad idea to force a Mistem to fight?"

The corners of my mouth twitch up. I know what I want to do, and now I have a perfect opportunity. "Thanks," I tell him. "I don't think I'll be joining your army, but I hope all goes well."

Roland's hand moves from my shoulder to grasp my hand. "I appreciate that."

A comfortable silence follows, but then the clamour of people preparing for war reaches us from another hallway. "You should go. You'll have a better chance if you're well-prepared when Mishfont gets here."

Roland kisses my hand before letting it go. "And what will you do?"

"I'll probably raid the library before heading home."

He nods and we part ways.

* * *

'Raid' is a good description of what I'm doing among the bookshelves. I tear through them, selecting any that might help me, especially those with maps. Some might call what I'm about to do *treason*, but it was never directly forbidden. Besides, as much as everyone else may disagree, I'm doing this for the benefit of the country.

I gather up everything I need, but I don't go just yet. I write a quick note to Roland, drip some wax from a candle at the bottom, and, taking my signet ring from my pocket, I press it into the hardening pool. I place it on the window seat where Roland and I sat when he first showed me this place, leaving it for him to find. I take one last look around my favorite room in the palace. How long it will be before I see these walls again, I don't know.

26

The Journey Begins

Skylar

When I get home, everyone is still at the table, waiting to hear what happened. Dumping my borrowed books on the table, I answer their questions before they can even ask.

"Mishfont's moving toward the border and our army is going to meet them in battle." Gasps, groans, and small, stifled screams are the response.

"Skylar, you're not . . . you don't have to . . . " Mom stammers.

"No, Mom. I don't have to fight and I won't." Mom's shoulders relax as she sighs in relief. "Not in the traditional way, at least." Mom's shoulders slump as she sighs in exasperation.

"What do you mean?" Dad demands. "What do those Haeltons want you to do?"

"Nothing," I respond, opening one of the books to a page covered by a map that shows both Vexenta and Mishfont. "I have my own battle plans."

"What battle plans?" Mandy asks. "What do you think you're going to do?"

"No one in the council, Roland included, thinks we could weaken Mishfont's army from the inside, make the king surrender or agree to a treaty, and finally put an end to this war. I intend to prove them wrong." I point to a spot on the map, a place in Mishfont some distance from our eastern border. "This is where the reports say the army is." I move my finger west along the page, heading towards a group of hills. "And this is the path it's taking. If I intercept it and sneak in I could—"

"Get yourself killed!" Mom exclaims. "Sweetheart, you're only one person. What could you do alone against an entire army? They'd know immediately that you aren't supposed to be there."

I shake my head. "They wouldn't notice or care about an extra Mistem wandering around." Confused expressions are the only response. "Mishfont's army uses Mistems."

"As servants?" Mandy asks.

I shake my head. "As soldiers." Still no one says a word, but they all stare at me in wide-eyed disbelief. "They use them to distract our soldiers during battle to give their Haelton fighters an advantage."

"But that's . . . using Mistems on a battlefield . . . it's . . . " Dad's so flustered he can hardly get the words out.

"See?" I say, gesturing towards him. "You're getting angry just thinking about it. Imagine how the ones who are actually in the battle feel! They'd be ready to leave, maybe even to rebel! I wouldn't be just one person once I get into the camp. I could get the other Mistems to join me and make things harder for the Haeltons."

"How would you even get across the border? You don't have a passport," Mom points out.

Reaching into my pocket, I pull out my signet ring and toss it onto the table. "This is the only passport I need."

Dad immediately grabs the ring then stares between it and me, seeming to memorize the seal, before passing it to Mom, who passes it to Mandy. All of them have the same reaction.

"How long . . . ?" Dad begins.

"Since my first visit to the palace after the megaline incident."

"He made you a noble?!" Mandy exclaims. "And you didn't tell us?!"

"I didn't want anyone to freak out over it." Mandy falls silent and I continue. "Anyway, this will allow me to get across the border."

Dad shakes his head. "Do you think the border guards would believe you when you show them that ring? They'd probably think you stole it."

"Probably, but they might believe that I'm a noble's servant. I see it happen all the time in the palace. If nobles want some product from Mishfont they'll send a servant over to get it and just give them a letter to show the guards. They only need to see an official seal at the bottom of the paper. No one expects a Mistem to cause trouble, so they usually get there and back without any problems. You should hear Lady Scarlett constantly bragging about all the fabrics and things she gets from Mishfont every other week."

"Even then, you're not making a journey like that alone." Dad pauses and takes a breath. "If you really need to do this, I'll go with you."

"No, Dad, you don't need to. I can go," Mandy offers.

My jaw drops. They're both offering to do this? I know they're concerned about my safety, and maybe they've given up trying to talk me out of it, but to go with me? I don't have time to think about this, though. Mishfont's army is getting closer every minute and if I'm going to have time to carry out my plan I need to leave as soon as I can.

"Look, if someone really needs to come with me, Mandy would be the best choice." I cut Dad off before he can protest. "You need to run the stand in the market. People in the village see you almost every day and if you were gone, they would notice. But they don't always see Mandy, so if she came with me it wouldn't be as obvious."

A long silence follows. Mom and Dad keep looking at each other, then between me, Mandy, and the map. Mom jerks her head toward their bedroom, and both of them retreat into it, leaving Mandy and I to stare at each other and wait. Then, as if the thought occurred to us both at exactly the same moment, we slip over to their closed door, pressing out ears against it the way we would at similar times when we were kids.

"Do you really want them doing this?" Dad's strained voice asks.

"You're the one who offered to go with her!"

"To buy us more time to talk her out of it!"

"I don't think it would work. Skylar said the *king* doesn't want her going, yet she's still trying to do this." Mom takes a shuddering breath. "Would you rather let her go when we can make sure she isn't alone, or have her sneaking off by herself in the middle of the night?"

"But to take Mandy . . . "

"Skylar is right, that would be less noticeable. They're both adults, and Mandy is a smart girl. She can help keep Skylar from being too impulsive." A pause. When Mom speaks again, she sounds near tears. "But still, I don't know. Are we going to lose our girls?"

"Skylar's a good fighter, it seems. And she wouldn't do anything that would put her in immediate danger, not with Mandy at risk too." Another pause. "Do you really think she'd sneak off if we don't let her go?"

"She's determined to do this. When have you ever seen Skylar give up when she's like this?"

"Only when she has no other choice." Dad gives a humourless laugh. "I think it would take more than one army to stop her." The sharp sound of fingers snapping reaches us, then Dad's whispers become more excited. "Maybe we don't need to stop her ourselves. The king might do that for us!"

"What?"

"You saw the way he looked at her today. He likes her! He wouldn't want anything to happen to her. He'll probably figure out what she's doing and bring her back!"

"Then what would we do?"

"Let them go. It will take them days to reach the army and by then King Roland will have probably tried to see her, and we can drop hints as to where she's gone. He's better equipped to stop her than we are."

After a moment, Mom mutters in agreement, then the sound of footsteps comes toward the door. Mandy and I dash back to the table, pretending we were studying the maps the whole time.

Our parents emerge from their bedroom and Dad clears his throat. "Alright, Skylar. I can see that there's no way we'll be able to stop you from doing this, but at least we can make sure you aren't going alone. You girls can go, just promise us you'll be careful and won't put yourselves in any more danger than you need to."

"We promise," Mandy and I say in unison.

"Mandy," Mom says. "We're counting on you to keep your sister out of trouble."

"I'll do my best," Mandy smiles nervously as I roll my eyes.

We immediately go to pack everything we need, which isn't much. We each take a small sack with a change of clothes and a blanket. We also take a bundle of empty sacks, so it looks like we're prepared to take a lot of extra stuff back with us. In one of the sacks I put a pouch full of coins to enhance the illusion. When we go back into the kitchen, Mom hands us a big basket filled with packages of food for the journey. I quickly write a letter to tell the border guards that *Lady Skylar of Vexenta is sending two of her maids into Mishfont to purchase the materials she requires for her wardrobe.* I try to make it look as official as possible before dripping some candle wax into it, pressing in the seal of my signet ring. Then I stuff the letter into the bag with the coins and stash the ring deep in my pocket. After a series of hugs and tearful goodbyes, we set out into the fading light.

27

The Plot Revealed

Roland

As soon as I have some time to myself, I slip over to the library. It's quiet and seems empty. "Skylar?" I call as I wander between the shelves. No answer. Maybe she's so enthralled with whatever book she's found that she didn't hear me. Or she's still angry and isn't responding. I search the shelves, noting that there are quite a few empty spots in the geography section.

I make my way toward the window seat she likes. As I approach, I call again. "Skylar?" Still no response. "Rose?" I try, hoping for any sort of reaction. Silence.

I reach the window seat and find it empty. The only sign that Skylar was here is a piece of paper folded on the bench. I pick it up and open it. There's only one word written on it: *Sorry*. I groan as it all clicks into place and stare at the note. At the bottom, mocking me, is a wax impression showing the seal from the ring I gave her. The gift I had hoped would win Skylar over is the very thing allowing her to disobey me now.

Sorry, she said. Somehow, I doubt she is. But she likely will be soon if I don't stop her. I don't have time to go myself, but I scribble a letter and summon a messenger.

"Yes, Sire?" he says when he arrives.

I hand him the letter. "Go to Lady Skylar's home as quickly as you can and give her this."

"Yes, Sire." He runs out and all I can do is continue my battle preparations while I wait.

* * *

In a couple of hours, the messenger returns. "Well?" I demand.

He quickly sticks his fidgeting hands behind his back. "The lady was not at her home, Your Majesty."

"Where is she, then?" My voice is harsher than I intended, trying to cover the surging panic.

"Her father told me she was running a small errand toward the east. I searched as far as I could in the time I had, but I saw no sign of her. I left the note with her parents."

A lot of good that will do. I dismiss the messenger with an impatient wave. I was too late. She's already left, and I have no way of stopping her. I can't send soldiers to search for her, not with the imminent battle. I certainly can't look for her myself. All I can do is try to fight this battle as soon as we can manage, put everyone on alert so she isn't accidently killed in the fight, and hope we can get to her before she gets herself into trouble.

28

The Journey

Skylar

Halfway through the night the moon disappears behind gathering clouds and Mandy and I decide to rest until the sun comes up. Our plan is to cross into Mishfont south of the hills and then head straight toward the path of the army. I try to hurry Mandy along before our parents can put their plan into action, but Mandy finds any excuse to slow down. Still, we make it to the border by the end of the day.

Guards from both Mishfont and Vexenta patrol the area. Mandy and I approach with our heads down, avoiding eye contact. A Mishfont guard stops us just before we leave Vexenta. "What's your business here?" he demands gruffly.

Without a word, we hand him the letter I wrote. I shoot glances up at him through my lashes as the guard reads over the letter and examines the seal at the bottom. "Skylar," he murmurs to himself. "Never heard of her before. *Hmph.* All these young new courtiers trying to impress." He hands back the letter but doesn't let us pass. "There's a five gold crossing tax you need to pay if you want to enter the country," he informs us with a slight smirk.

"I never heard about that," I mutter, raising my head a bit. Mandy elbows me in the ribs.

"We can't argue," she whispers so only I can hear. But the guard heard me, and his smirk becomes a scowl.

"There's probably a lot you don't know. And that tax can be doubled if you're going to give me attitude." Clenching my fists in my pocket, I step back and let Mandy give him the money. Seeming satisfied, he steps aside and we hurry past.

When we're out of earshot I turn to Mandy. "You realize he was lying, right? He was just getting us to bulk up his salary because we had no other choice."

"I know, but we can't get into a fight if we want to go unnoticed. This is exactly why Mom and Dad wanted someone with you."

With a grunt of annoyance, I let the topic drop and fish out a book from my bag. I flip it open to a map of Mishfont and think out loud as I examine it. "Okay, so we just crossed the border here . . . " I point to a spot at the edge of the map, "and the army is somewhere around here . . . " my finger circles an area north-east of where we are, "so we need to go . . . " I look around us, searching for any landmarks from the map and noting the position of the sun, "that way," I point slightly to the left of the direction we're heading. We start off in that direction, turning away from the road that leads to cities further south.

* * *

We move as quickly as the rocky terrain will let us. We don't need to worry about staying hidden, since we never run into anyone else among the bare hills. It seems that no one ever comes this way, so when we hear the sounds of a crowd in the distance after days of lonely trudging, we know we've reached the army.

We come to the edge of a wooded area and, hidden among the trees, we watch the well-coordinated set up of a military camp as the sun drifts toward the horizon. It's easy to distinguish ranks and pick out who the important people are from the type of armour they wear. There's a sizable cluster that really stands out from the rest. They wear thin leather armour, pale faces peaking out from beneath their helmets. The Mistems.

Ever since I heard about the Mistems in the Mishfont army I've wondered why they didn't just sneak away in the middle of the night. The reason becomes apparent as the camp forms. The Mistems are all crowded into a spot near the centre of the army, surrounded by Haelton soldiers. Guards taking their turn on watch duty make constant circles around the group, swords drawn, sending a clear message: anyone who tries to desert won't survive the attempt. This makes our job more difficult.

"How are we supposed to get in now?" Mandy asks, a note of panic creeping into her voice.

I put a hand on her shoulder, trying to calm her down. "Let's just watch and wait until it's dark. Maybe we can figure something out."

We find a comfortable spot in the undergrowth where we're invisible to the army but can still watch what's going on. As we wait, we finish off the food Mom gave us. At least it's something to do.

The sky grows darker, and I start to notice something. Every so often, Haelton officers will get Mistem soldiers to run errands for them. Usually this seems to involve some wagons at the edge of the camp where a Haelton guard will hand the soldiers items from inside one of them for the officer. Supply wagons. I turn to Mandy, who's looking in a different direction. "Mandy!" She jumps at the sudden break in the silence and her head whips around to face me. I grin at her. "I have an idea!" In a low voice, I explain my plan.

"Do you really think it will work?" she asks when I finish.

"There's only one way to find out," I reply.

* * *

When the sun has completely disappeared and campfires provide the only light, Mandy and I put my plan into action. We hide the empty food basket and stow the rest of our stuff in our bags. We sneak around the perimeter of the camp until we come to the line of supply wagons.

Only two guards watch them. The first is pacing back and forth at one end of the line, the second is leaning against a wagon at the other end, watching a group around the fire closest to him and smiling at the jokes and stories they pass around. We go to his end of the line and quickly dart to the back of one wagon. Keeping my head as low as I can so that I stay out of view, I peer into it. It's filled with crates that have names of various foods marked on them. Not what we need. I turn to Mandy, shake my head, and point toward the next one. We creep over.

We continue doing this until we come to a wagon littered with weapons, shields, and spare pieces of armour. I nod to Mandy and we silently climb into it. Just as I had hoped, Mishfont's army has a stash of spare supplies in case something is broken or lost before the battle. We piece together two full sets of leather armour, put them on, then stuff our things into military-issued packs. Now we're indistinguishable from the Mistem soldiers. Just in time.

"What are you two doing in here?!" We both jump at the voice and turn to see that the guard who was watching the fireside antics has returned to his patrol. "What are you doing?" he repeats with a nasty growl.

"O-orders, sir," I stammer out, trying to recover from the surprise. "We were told to put some extra supplies back in here."

"W-we thought you were watching something important and didn't want to disturb you," Mandy adds. It's perfect. We look innocent and obedient while the guard has a hard choice to make. Does he report us and admit that he wasn't doing his job well enough to stop us, or does he let us go and pretend this never happened? His jaw clenches and his eyes dart between us while Mandy and I lower our heads.

Soon he decides on the safer option. "Get back to your tents," he snaps, stepping back so we can jump down from the wagon. He watches as we dash towards the Mistem area.

I turn back to see him pacing around the wagons, his head now frequently whipping around in every direction. I grin at Mandy and she smiles back while heaving a sigh of relief. We did it. We've penetrated into the heart of the Mishfont army.

29

The Mist Legion

Skylar

M ost of the soldiers have gone to sleep, but a few still sit around the fires that have been left to burn themselves out. Heads turn as we step into the dying light. Some study us with intent gazes. A girl with wavy hair pulled back into a stubby knot gets up and strides over, eyes narrowed.

"I don't think I've ever seen you two around before," she greets.

"We just came from one of the outposts," I reply, just as frankly. "We were sent with a message that more troops are coming."

The girl raises her eyebrows and crosses her arms while looking us up and down. "I see . . . " she pauses, then suddenly asks, "Are you with ML?"

Mandy and I both hesitate, having no idea how to respond.

"The Legion?" the girl elaborates unhelpfully, her brows turning down in a scowl. I nod, hoping it's the right answer. It doesn't seem to do anything. "Okay . . . " she challenges. "Tell me what legion I mean."

Neither of us can answer. I glance around at the other Mistems sitting by their fires, watching the interaction, and all I see are more suspicious glares directed at us as they whisper to each other.

When we don't respond, the girl turns on her heel. "Come with me," she says over her shoulder, starting towards one of the tents. I turn to Mandy and she nods, eyes darting nervously to the faces staring at us. We follow the girl.

She leads us to a tent in the middle of the Mistem area and pulls the flap aside. "Captain?" she says, poking her head inside.

"Come in," a gruff voice answers. The girl ducks into the tent, motioning for us to follow. But we stop just outside the tent entrance, peering in through the half-open door. Inside, there are four Mistems seated in a circle on the ground, facing each other. The girl who led us here seems to be addressing the man sitting almost directly in front of the door. He appears to be the same age as Dad, but it's hard to tell. His face is hard and stern and there are lines around his eyes and mouth that form a permanent scowl. He reminds me of a statue, worn down and aged by constant, violent storms. "What is it?" he asks over his shoulder, making no effort to hide the annoyance in his voice.

"A couple of girls just came into the camp, Captain," she replies. "I don't think they're from our group."

"Where are they?" he demands.

The girl turns around and, seeing that we didn't come in with her, gestures to the door. "Right out there."

"Well, bring them in here!"

She quickly sticks her head out the door, glaring at us and motioning for us to come in. Mandy hesitates, almost taking a step back, but I grab her arm and pull her into the tent with me. Something tells me that if we want the Mistems to go along with our plan, this is the person to talk to.

The group shifts as we enter, making room and turning so they can examine us. The girl who brought us here backs into a corner, pressing her back against the tent walls, while Mandy and I stoop slightly under the low roof.

"Who are you? Where are you from?" the captain demands, staring straight into our eyes. I try to think of a good way to explain, but he has no patience. When neither of us answer immediately he turns to his companions. "Search their bags," he instructs. Two of them stand up and yank the packs we got from the supply wagon off our backs before sitting down again and rummaging through them, listing their contents aloud.

"Empty sacks."

"Money. Looks like quite a bit of it," one says, pulling out the coin purse I brought and weighing it in his hand.

"Clothes—these aren't army-issued."

"There's a note in this one!" the soldier holding my bag exclaims, holding up the letter I wrote to show the border guards. The captain takes it and reads it, his eyes lingering at the bottom of the page, examining the seal.

"So . . ." he says thoughtfully, glancing back at us. "We have a couple of girls from Vexenta, maids, running away from their mistress, this–" he looks back at the letter, "Lady Skylar. And you thought an enemy army would be a good place to hide because . . . ?" his eyes turn back to us as he lets the sentence trail off.

"We're not running away from anything and we fully intend to return home eventually," I say immediately. One of the captain's eyebrows shoots up in a quizzical and disbelieving expression. Similar looks appear on the other faces clustered into the tent. I go on. "That letter was meant to mislead the border guards. My sister and I have never worked for any Haelton nobles. But we know what's been going on in the war and we're as sick of it as anyone else who can see past the false predictions and glorious delusions of the no-bility. We want it to stop, and we figured that, with the battle coming and an army half-full of Mistems being forced to fight heading towards our borders, this would be a good place to start forming a resistance."

The captain regards me with an amused, curious half-smirk. "You're not normal, are you?" he asks, his expression becoming something close to a smile.

I half-smile in return. "I've been told I'm not."

The captain turns to the other Mistems, seeming to ask a silent question. They all nod in response, then he turns back to me. "I admire your taking action like this, but I'm afraid you're a bit late to *start* a resistance."

"You've already formed one?"

He nods. "Do you think they call me *Captain* because I'm actually an officer? No, I'm the captain of the Mist Legion, a group of pretty much every Mistem in the army, with plans to break away from Haelton control. Seeing as you went to all this trouble to help, you're welcome to join. As long as," he adds, holding up a warning finger, "you can assure us that you won't be a hindrance."

"You don't need to worry about that," I assure him. The captain looks doubtful, but he invites us to sit.

"Tell me, can either of you fight?" he asks. "You need to look like you've been in the army for a while, so you don't draw any unwanted attention."

"I can," I say immediately. The captain sits back, seeming surprised by how quickly I answer. Mandy silently shakes her head, but no one takes any notice.

"Well," the captain regards me quizzically as he stands, "if you're so confident in your abilities, let's test them."

We all shuffle out of the tent into a clear area around one of the dying fires. The captain emerges after the rest of us, holding what look like two large wooden daggers. "They don't give us real weapons unless we're about to go into a battle, but we're allowed to have these to practice," he tells me when I look at them curiously. The girl who took us to the captain heads over to the people she was sitting with before we came and starts talking to them excitedly. Meanwhile, the captain looks at the people around us.

"We have a couple new recruits," he announces, just loud enough for those at the closest fires to hear. "I need a volunteer to test them in a duel."

"I'll do it," offers one girl, standing from her place at a fire to my right. She looks a few years older than Mandy, her straight white hair cut short, just below her ears. The captain nods and hands a sword to me and my opponent. While everyone backs away to give us room, we face each other, our stances wide and dagger-swords at the ready. I'm careful to hold my sword exactly the way I was shown in the palace training sessions.

When the captain gives us the signal to fight, I don't move, expecting my opponent to make the first attack and getting ready to block. But she doesn't move either. In fact, she steps back, holding her sword in a blocking position. I take a tentative step forward. She backs up again. I take another step toward her and she darts to the side. Every time I make any sort of advance, even though I never actually attack, she dodges, hardly ever getting within reach. I feel more like a child playing tag than a soldier in a duel. After a few minutes, I get tired of it and start moving faster. My opponent darts away as quickly as I come near her and we end up just running around the ring created by watching spectators. Then I take a swing at her. She's startled by my sudden attack and hesitates, giving me a chance to get within reach. I swing, then back off. She blocks and backs away. I advance again, slicing my sword high this time so that she raises hers to block me. As she steps back, sword still raised, I dash beside her, placing the point of my weapon behind her leg so she trips over it, throwing her off balance. One last hit to the base of her wooden blade sends my opponent to the ground and the sword flying from her hand.

I straighten and turn to the spectators, pleased. I'm not sure what I was expecting. Applause, approval, an impressed captain saying I was right about my abilities. I didn't expect the stunned silence that follows my victory. Everywhere I look around the circle I meet the same wide-eyed expressions. I turn back to my opponent, who's still sitting on the ground, and see her looking at me the same way. "Are you alright?" I ask, holding out my hand to help her up. Before she can respond or take my hand, someone seizes my shoulder and pulls me away, so suddenly that I drop my sword.

The captain takes me back to his tent and doesn't let go of me until we're inside. Then he rounds on me, his surprise turned to anger. "What was that?!" he demands.

"What do you mean? You asked if I could fight, I showed you I can."

"You fight like a Haelton! Do you think the officers aren't going to find that strange? The last thing we need is to have them keeping a closer eye on us. It could ruin everything!" The captain turns away from me, breathing hard. When he turns back, a scowl covers his face. "Tell me, if you never worked for a Haelton, like you claim, how did you learn to fight like that? How did you even know the army was here? This is supposed to be a surprise attack. I doubt it would have become common knowledge, even if Vexenta's nobility found out."

I meet his angry gaze. "Remember that letter you found in my bag, the one written by Lady Skylar?"

"You learned from her?" he demands.

I reach into my pocket and pull out my signet ring, holding it out so the captain can see it. "I *am* her."

The captain snatches the ring from my hand, then seizes the letter from on top of my bag, where a soldier placed it when we left the tent. He stands for a moment, comparing the seal on the page with my ring, then looking back at me. "Did you steal this?" he finally asks.

"No. Do you think that if I were a thief on the run I would try to hide in a place where I'm surrounded by Haelton soldiers?"

"Then where did you get this?"

"King Roland gave it to me himself."

"He gave you a title?" the captain asks, disbelief lacing his voice. "Why?"

"I met the king, he found me interesting, and he invited me to the palace. I started talking about things that should be changed in our country, he seemed to see my point, and suggested I get involved in politics. Then he decided that if I was going to be involved with the court, I should have a title." I respond with a blank tone, reducing the story to its barest essentials.

The captain laughs humourlessly. "He *seemed* to agree with you." He glances again between the ring and me, a grimace somewhere between pity and disgust crossing his face. "I see what this is. You're the royal brat's pet!"

My fists clench. "*Excuse me?!*"

The captain hardly seems to notice my reaction. "Tell me if this sounds familiar," he says, contemplatively turning my ring over in his hand. "Some rich, important Haelton finds a normal girl and decides he likes her, for whatever reason. Looks, attitude, whatever piques his interest. He decides he wants to keep her around and invites her to stay with him, giving her presents, saying whatever she wants to hear, anything to make her feel special and happy to stick around him like a puppy. Until he gets tired of her and the illusion crumbles." The captain meets my eyes with a meaningful gaze. "It happens. I've seen it a few times and heard about it even more. Maybe you didn't, maybe you were sheltered before now, but welcome to the real world."

Another voice speaks before I can reply.

"Do the rich guys usually try to kill their pets the day they meet?" I whip around as the captain looks up, startled. Neither of us had noticed Mandy standing in the doorway. She marches in, eyes blazing. "You think we've never seen what the real world can be?" she demands of the captain. She grabs my right arm and undoes the strap holding the sleeve of the leather armour closed over it. When she pulls the sleeve aside, revealing the long, red lines imprinted on my upper arm, the captain's eyes widen. Mandy jerks my arm closer to him, her voice rising almost to a shout. "This is what the king did to her when she stood up to him! He threw her in the arena with knightcrawlers and she got these scars fighting them off and escaping! And after all that, after she repeatedly tried to push him away and went against him, he still wanted her around and he still gave her that ring. Is that what Haeltons normally do when they want a pet?"

There's a long pause where no one moves. Eventually, the captain shakes his head and I yank my arm back from Mandy, lacing the sleeve up again. "It doesn't really matter what she is, though," the captain says. "If she keeps fighting like a Haelton, it'll draw unwanted attention to us."

"Then, in the future, I'll try pretending to be scared of my own shadow like everyone else," I snap.

The captain grabs my shoulder and pulls me toward him. He speaks quietly, but his voice is loud in my ear. "You might think you have some new-found power where you come from, but here you're just like every other Mistem: nothing. Learn to at least act like you know your place or everything we've worked for, every plan we've made, is doomed to fail before they even start." He shoves me away, dropping my ring at my feet before heading for the door of the tent. "Grab your stuff," he orders without looking back at us. "We'll find a tent for you to stay in."

30

Battle Plans

Skylar

I awake to officers shouting for everyone to get up and prepare to move out. We spend most of the day marching eastward, never breaking from our closely formed ranks. Soldiers will sometimes break up the monotony of marching by talking to those near them. Now and then a particularly bored or excited group of Haeltons will break out in a marching or battle song, until an officer gets annoyed and silences them.

Late in the afternoon we stop to make camp. After the tents are set up, everyone breaks into duelling groups to train. Mandy and I quickly find ourselves alone.

"Come on," I say to Mandy, heading toward the supply of wooden swords. "I'll teach you some moves." A high-pitched noise like a stifled yelp makes both our heads turn. Staring at us, aghast, is my opponent from last night. "*Blocking* moves," I emphasize, looking straight into her eyes. She turns and quickly walks away.

With a determined stride I go with Mandy to get the swords, then we find an open area to practice in. I tutor her on how to hold the weapon and ward off attacks, then we watch the other Mistems as they duel before trying it ourselves. Mostly they circle each other, swords ready. Occasionally one person will step towards another, taking a half-swing, but will rapidly jump back while they're opponent moves to block or dodge the blow that never comes.

Most of the Haeltons ignore us, focussing on their own training. But every so often a few of them will take a break and watch us. Some will take a swing at an unsuspecting Mistem just to watch them scramble to defend themselves. As Mandy and I practice, making an effort to blend in with the rest, one Haelton targets me. I step away from an advance and feel a wooden blade poke me in the back. Spinning around, I look up just in time to see the sword careening toward my head. I raise my own blade and ward off the blow before darting backwards. After a brief glance toward the soldier grinning at me, I remember my promise to the captain and turn my gaze downwards. I focus on the sword he's twirling in his hand, waiting to see what he'll do. He swings it suddenly, making me jump to avoid it, before walking away, laughing. *Just wait.* It's become my mantra since we arrived. *Just wait.*

Behind me, Mandy releases her breath in a long sigh. "Good, he's gone." I raise my eyes to glare after the retreating back of the Haelton before a wall of other soldiers hides him from view. "Come on, Skylar, forget it." Pause. "It looks like everyone's starting to get ready for supper. Let's just go get something to eat."

"Fine."

We return our swords to the supply pile, then wander around the fires, looking for a group we can join. Most of them don't notice us, or pretend not to, until one voice speaks up. "Hey, new girls! Over here!" The girl who first spoke to us last night is waving us over.

I thank her for letting us join her as we sit down and she hands us bowls of food, but she just shrugs. "I'm Skylar, by the way," I tell her, and Mandy introduces herself too.

"I'm Amy, but I already knew who you were," she says, looking at me.

"Really?"

She nods. "Everyone does," she states, then, at a sharp look from me, clarifies. "Every Mistem. Word goes around fast through ML."

"Hmm."

"Everyone knows quickly but the family," Mandy mutters.

I'm about to reply when Amy speaks up again. "Did your king really give you a signet ring?" I sigh and dig into my pocket, handing the ring to her to inspect. She turns it over and over, light from the fire catching on it in flashes. "I've never known anything like this to happen before. The captain said you had this, but—"

"Where is the captain, anyway?" I ask, changing the subject.

Amy hands my ring back and I quickly stow it away. "In his tent, finalizing plans for the battle."

"So, what is the plan? We haven't heard anything about it yet."

"Most of us haven't. If too many people were involved in making the plans it would get suspicious. If they need you, they call you in, but otherwise word gets passed around when everything is decided."

"Oh."

"I don't think it will be long now. I heard an officer say we were close."

I open my pack and dig through it until I find the book I'm looking for. I draw it out, under Amy's curious gaze, and flip through it to the map. "Let's see, where are we?" I muse aloud.

"Somewhere near this village, I think," Mandy says, pointing. "I saw it off in the distance while we were marching today."

"Then we're probably around here," I say, pointing to a spot along the army's path, then I trace my finger in a line from there to the hills. "That can't take more than a day or two to travel."

Amy, who was leaning over the book, sits back. "Then we should hear something tomorrow."

We finish eating mostly in silence, though Amy asks about Vexenta. Mandy tells tales of home cheerily, but I'm careful about what I say, especially when talking about Roland, considering how fast news spreads in the camp. I'm rescued when someone I recognize from the captain's tent comes and tells me I'm needed.

I stand to go, but Mandy hesitates. "Coming?" I ask.

"She didn't say they needed me."

"So?" Mandy smiles, gets up, and we head off with promises to Amy that we'll come back.

In the captain's tent, he motions for us to sit down. "Everything is mostly settled for the battle, but we wanted to ask about Vexenta's plans, seeing as we have someone here who knows the nobility personally."

"Sure, what's the plan?"

"While the Haeltons are focused on crossing the border, we'll fall back and then rush at them from behind. They won't expect it, we can move fast enough that they won't have time to react, and if we can take out the army before it gets well across the border, we won't have to deal with Vexenta's army."

I shake my head. "You'll have to contend with Vexenta if we're anywhere near the hills during the attack. The plan was to have as many soldiers as possible on those hills within a week. It's been about that long since we left. If you attack your own army within sight of the border, Vexenta will take advantage of the chaos and you'll be breaking away from one group of Haeltons only to be taken over by another a few minutes later."

The captain considers this, giving opportunity for others to talk. "But what else can we do?" someone asks no one in particular.

"Couldn't we fight Vexenta too?"

"Yeah! Isn't the point of this to show Haeltons, *all* Haeltons, that we're not scared and weak the way they think we are?"

"And you think you can defeat two well-trained Haelton armies to do it?" I interject.

"We need to try something," the captain returns darkly. "To be the ones on top for a change and give them a taste of what they've done to us for years. We'll show them we're capable of turning it back on them!"

"If we do the exact same things as the people we're fighting, are we really any better than they are?" I pause, waiting for what they'll say. When the response is blank stares, I continue. "The Haeltons aren't going to let us take their positions of power easily. Yes, we may surprise them with a sudden attack, but then they'll fight back. They outnumber us. We need to get their attention in a different way, one they won't expect or have seen before."

"How? Haeltons only pay attention to displays of strength."

"And there are ways to show it without fighting."

"Like what?"

In my mind I'm taken back to the palace, to my room there, and Lady Millicent trying to stare me down, asking the same question. I didn't answer her then, I just stood my ground, refusing to back down. A smile creeps to my lips as an idea crystalizes in my head. I meet the captain's eyes. "We'll win the fight by not fighting."

A flood of confused faces looks back at me. "Skylar, are you alright?" Mandy asks. "This is weird even for you."

I launch into an explanation of my idea. Most of the Mist Legion officers are skeptical, but the captain nods slowly. "It's worth trying," he tells the group, a hesitant smile forming.

31

This is how it Ends

Skylar

T he next day's march is much the same as yesterday's, but with one difference: every Mistem is talking about the same thing. It started with
everyone who was in the tent last night giving the details of the plan to
those walking near them, then those people passed it on, and so on until
my idea has spread through the group like wildfire. A fire that abruptly
hits a barrier before the Haeltons can notice it. The Mistems here obviously do this a lot.

When we stop for the day, just beyond the shadow of the border hills,
everyone trains with renewed determination. Mandy and I are suddenly a
lot more popular, and it seems everyone wants to talk to us.

But the night is one of the longest I've ever had. I lie awake long after
everyone else is asleep, staring at the cloth ceiling of the tent the captain
found for us to share. Frustrated, I roll over with a soft groan. "Skylar?"
Mandy's whispered voice comes out of the darkness. "You're awake?"

"You too?" I reply.

"I keep thinking about tomorrow."

"Yeah, so do I."

There's a rustle as Mandy shifts, turning to face me. "What if it doesn't
work? What if they don't listen to us?" she says in a rush.

"They will, they'll have to." I'm reassuring myself as much as her. "I
know Roland will, at least."

"He's not really the one I'm worried about. Mishfont has a king who's
going to be in the battle, too."

"I know."

"And we don't know what he's like."

"Like every other Haelton with power," our tent-mate mumbles, only half-awake. "Now get some sleep if you want to have any chance of convincing *him* to do anything."

Mandy and I fall silent, but sleep still doesn't come easily.

* * *

As we eat breakfast early the next morning, a shouted command spreads through the camp. "Pack up and grab your weapons! We're entering Vexenta!"

I pack quickly, just before a weapon-loaded supply wagon rolls into the Mistem area. We each receive a real sword, the same size as the wooden training ones, and a small, rectangular shield barely wider than my forearm and only half the length of those the Haelton soldiers carry. We're about to get into marching formation when a Haelton, probably a scout, runs toward the camp from the direction of the hills. A few minutes later, new commands pass through the troops.

"Vexenta has an army waiting for us! Battle formations!"

From a distance, I catch the captain's eye. *I told you,* I mouth. He rolls his eyes before we're caught in the rush of soldiers moving into position. Three sections of Haelton soldiers in bright, metal armour, separated by two chunks of leather-clad Mistems.

By the time we're marching onto the open ground at the foot of the hills, the sun is shining strongly, glinting blindingly off the Haeltons. The last wisps of early-morning mist still hold their ground.

Flashes of light on the hills tell us where Vexenta's soldiers are. Small clusters of these flashes quickly come together and are joined by new ones until the whole stretch of hills are topped by a long, blazing strip. Then, with distant shouts and a roar of thundering footfalls, the strip hurtles toward us! Mishfont responds with the same shouts. The command of "CHARGE!" echoes above the din.

As the two armies rush towards each other, about to collide, we give our own signal. I raise my shield above my head and, in the other clump of Mistems, the captain does the same. We surge forward, our lighter armour and years of running from danger allowing us to pull in front of the Haelton soldiers. Officers yell, "Get back here!" but we ignore them, running ahead until we're halfway between the armies. Then we group together, forming two lines, one facing each army, our backs touching those across from us, shoulders touching those beside us, and shields and swords firmly held in front of us. A solid wall of Mistems.

The frontline soldiers of both armies skid to a halt when they reach the solid mass blocking the way, their comrades behind them colliding into their backs. They beat at us with their shields, some slice with their swords, but we block every blow they aim at us, pushing them back and standing our ground. Eventually, the shout of "Enough!" rings from both sides.

All the soldiers take two steps back. On the Mishfont side, someone steps forward from the middle of the crowd. His armour looks like gold, though I know it's bronze, and his helmet has a crown shape molded into the top of it. He raises his visor, revealing a face that's about ten years older than Roland's and contorted with rage. "WHAT IS THE MEANING OF THIS?!" he demands, his head whipping back and forth as he looks along the line in front of him, daring someone to speak.

The line parts in the middle. I step into the opening, in full view of everyone. Mishfont's king glares at me, holding his sword ready to strike. I stand tall, making myself look as strong and confident as possible, holding his gaze. Then I turn, looking between both armies.

"This needs to end now!" I shout to the crowds. Murmurs run through both armies. On the Vexenta side I see some familiar faces that don't look very surprised to see me. Lady Lauretta gives me a weak half smile when our eyes meet. I notice Lady Millicent leaning on her sword, the point stuck into the ground, a bored look plastered on her face.

My attention is pulled back to the other army by the king. "What?" he asks in a dangerous tone. I continue addressing the armies.

"How many years have our countries been fighting like this? How many years have been spent struggling for land, power, or some promise of glory? How many people, friends and family members, have been lost?" I pause, giving a moment for my words to take effect.

"And what has been gained from all of that?" I continue. I wait, seeing if anyone will answer. No one does. "I'll tell you what's been gained: nothing! In decades of fighting neither country has made any real progress into the other's territory. Sure, some places have been captured, but they've always been taken back later! This war is going nowhere, and nothing is ever going to come of it!

"What are you trying to gain? Whatever wealth you think the other country has? There seems to be plenty of riches in each already; you don't need more. What are you trying to prove? Which country is stronger? I'd say it's a tie, and that's not going to change. Aren't there other ways of proving this if it's really necessary? This war is nothing but pointless waste and it needs to stop. Now."

I make a show of holding my sword high above my head, letting the sun glance off the metal, then I throw it down hard. All along the line of Mistems there's the clatter and thumps of falling swords. "We are fed up with it, and we refuse to fight a useless battle any longer. We've made our decision, what will you do?"

A low buzz of discussion fills the air as soldiers from both sides re-act to what I said. I scan the crowds. Some faces are skeptical, others confused or conflicted, but I see small nods scattered among the rows of heads, faces with sorrowful or thoughtful looks. But Mishfont's king hardly seems affected.

"You turn my Mistems against me, then put yourself between two armies just to say this? Are you stupid, girl?"

"Stubborn, yes," a familiar voice says behind me. "Stupid? Not quite."

I spin around to see Roland, in armour much like that of Mishfont's king, staring at me and shaking his head, a restrained smile on his face. I grin at him before he turns to the other king. "I'll admit she has some good points, ones we've been ignoring."

"You're listening to a Mistem," the other king scoffs.

"I'm listening to what the people have to say. The people who do most of the daily work that keeps our countries running."

With a sneer, the king of Mishfont turns to me, pointing his sword. "If you want any chance of surviving the day, you'll get back in your ranks."

Roland steps toward me, protectively holding his sword ready. "She's one of my citizens and you have no right to make such threats."

His gaze flicks between me and Roland. "You're sure she's from your country?"

"Quite. You might have noticed that Skylar isn't easy to overlook." He smiles at me.

I return the smile. "When I want to be, Roland."

Ignoring me, Mishfont's king turns to Roland. "So, what? You want to call off the battle now?"

"I think," Roland responds in a measured tone, "that we can find a more productive solution to our issues."

Determined not to be ignored, I step forward. "A treaty, for instance. Or, if you insist on having a violent solution—"

"THAT'S ENOUGH FROM YOU!" the king yells, now enraged. He charges toward me, his sword flashing as he swings it. I back up quickly, starting to dive for my near-forgotten sword. But before I can reach it, something else streaks in front of me with a resounding clash of metal on metal.

From behind my raised shield, I watch Roland and Mishfont's king engage in a furious battle. They're moving so fast it's hard to see what they're doing. The sound of their blows striking each other's shields and swords creates a loud percussion symphony that rings across the battlefield. Soldiers from both armies come closer to watch, some cheering on their king, though none step in to help.

Then a sword falls to the ground, closely followed by the king of Mishfont. His helmet is knocked halfway off his head. Roland stands over him, his sword poised to strike. He's aiming for the other king's neck.

Roland is going to kill him.

"Roland!" My voice is little more than a whisper, but he still hears me. He pauses. The world seems to freeze, with everyone holding their breath. Roland's eyes flick over to my face for just a moment, then they're back on the other king.

Slowly, Roland lowers his sword, pointing it at the other king's neck but not slicing. "Do you want to reconsider your response?" he demands of the man on the ground.

Mishfont's king has no choice. Either he accepts a truce or Roland kills him, winning the battle and possibly the war.

The king in the dirt nods slowly, carefully avoiding the tip of Roland's sword. It moves away from him as Roland sheathes it. After a brief hesitation, Roland holds out his hand to help the other man up. Skeptically, he takes it. Then the world unfreezes in a flurry of activity and shouting as the two kings order their armies to return to their camps. Mishfont's Mistems skirt around their king, heading back a short distance away from the other soldiers.

As the armies start to move, Roland looks at me, smiling widely. I return his smile just as Mandy rushes up and embraces me.

Epilogue

Skylar

I'm at home, flat on my back on my bed, a book hovering over my head. My signet ring taps against it as I drum my fingers along the cover. I'm resting after collecting some much-needed berries this morning. I'm also recovering from the late night yesterday. Mandy and I arrived home after sunset and were immediately trapped in the embraces of our angrily relieved parents. Then, of course, we had to relay the entire story of our trip for the next few hours.

Mandy comes in, removing her flour-covered apron. "What are you reading?" she asks casually.

"A book I got from Roland's library."

"Another one? You must have read half of that library by now."

I smirk at her, glancing under the pages. "Some day I need to show you that place."

"Sure," is her response. "Anyway, could I trouble you to borrow a few coins?" *I knew it!*

"What for?"

"Mom wants me to bring some stuff to Dad . . . "

"Yeah . . . ?"

"And there's someone I want to talk to in the marketplace, but I need an excuse to visit his stand."

I sit up immediately, the book thumping closed on the bed in front of me. "Who is he?!" I demand.

"I don't have to tell you anything."

I put my right hand on top of the book, the seal of my ring facing up. "Don't you?"

Mandy walks over and pats my head. "No, little sister, I don't."

I swat her hand away. "Then I don't have to give you anything."

A shadow passes over Mandy's face. "Fine, if you want me to be lonely for the rest of my life. Just because you don't have to worry about it, having Roland and everything . . . "

I shove my hand into my book pile, knocking a few onto the floor, take out a hidden coin purse, and throw it at her. "Happy?"

She gives me a quick hug before skipping off. "Thanks, you're the best."

"Yeah, yeah."

As Mandy leaves the room and I pick up my book again, a knock sounds at the door. Mandy's voice drifts through the walls. "I've got it."

I'm just settling down again when the door opens and a familiar voice says, "Good afternoon."

"Oh, hello, I—Skylar!" Mandy calls.

With a sigh, I close the book again, keeping my finger in the page, and walk out of the room. Roland's at the door, watching me with a grin. "Enjoying the book?" he asks.

"I could enjoy it more without so many interruptions."

He gives me a sympathetic look. "Sorry. But I was hoping you would join me for a walk."

"I think that would be alright . . . " I look over at Mom, working industriously at the counter.

"As long as you're back in time for dinner, I don't mind."

"Alright then." I place my book on the table and head for the door. Roland offers me his right arm, in true gentlemanly fashion, and I hook my left through it. As the door closes behind us, we head down the path to the marshes. The area seems surprisingly empty. "You came by yourself today?"

"Yes, it's just the two of us. Is that alright?"

"Yes, it's fine." There's a pleasant pause, with the silence broken only by the sounds of nature and our feet treading along the path, before I ask, "Was there something you wanted to talk about?"

"Yes. Mishfont's king is coming to the palace in a few days with some officials. And leaders of the Mist Legion. We have a lot to sort out. I think you should be there."

"Of course, I'll be there."

"I'm still not happy that you went against me like that . . . "

I snort. "As if I'm happy with all recent events."

"But I must admit, it's made more progress with international relations than there has been for years."

I put my head closer to his shoulder, smiling up at him through my eyelashes. "So, I'm forgiven?"

He smiles down at me. "I can overlook it." There's another pause, and Roland's face clouds over. "Those recent events . . . You mean things like the arena incidents?"

I step away, taken aback by the sudden change in tone. "We don't really need to talk about them . . . "

"You brought it up." He sighs. "I really am sorry, Skylar. I was angry and intrigued and I wasn't thinking straight—"

I cut him off by putting my right hand on his arm. "I know," I say with a smile.

He looks down at my hand. "You're wearing the ring."

I take my hand back, holding it between us, watching the sun shine off the metal in a pinkish hallow. "I am."

He puts his hand under mine, his fingers brushing my wrist. The sun shines off his signet ring, too. He gazes into my eyes. "Does this mean you could forgive me?"

I place my hand is his, watching as the hallows of our rings blend into one. "I already have."